DEVIL'S CUT

IMMORTAL KEEPER VAMPIRE SERIES

L.A. MCGINNIS

ISBN-13: 978-1-970112-28-3
ISBN-13: 978-1-970112-32-0

Published in the United States of America by Fools Journey Press, 2021

Please visit my website at www.lamcginnis.com

"Whisky, like a beautiful woman,
demands attention.

You gaze first, then it's time to drink"

Haruki Murakami

1

LANGSTON-FORGE DISTILLERY'S BOARDROOM

"Selena, you *must* sign these," Emerson urged gently, leaning in so the other men couldn't overhear. "There's no options left."

I looked at the documents my lawyer had set in front of me, then lifted my gaze high enough to skim the faces of the board of directors seated around the table—a table *my* great-grandfather brought from Scotland—while trying to rein in my anger.

I was so goddamned pissed at the whole situation. At my father. At the board for pushing this takeover, right when the company—*and me*—were at their most vulnerable. But mostly, I was pissed at my brother.

I was twenty years old with the weight of the world on my shoulders, and everything was about to come crashing down. I picked up the pen, set the point to the paper, then hedged, as if I believed there was a chance—

"What if I ask for another extension?"

I knew that'd never happen, but I wanted to hear my lawyer say it out loud, because once I heard there was no hope, I could move forward with my crazy—maybe suicidal

—plan. Someone across the table impatiently cleared his throat as I hesitated. I'd never learned to play chess, but I did know how to read a room, and these men were glad I'd failed.

"You know as well as I do that the bank won't grant another extension. They've already given you far more leeway than usual." Emerson Holloway had been Granddad's lawyer, then Dad's, and now he was mine. He might be old, but he knew his shit, and always told me straight. Unlike the rest of the vultures gathered around this table, practically salivating at the prospect of the company going under.

While my mind grappled with the utter finality of signing away my family's company, my mouth desperately bargained. "Three days. Give me three more days and I'll fix this." God, I sounded like an addict. Maybe I was. "If I can't raise enough working capital, I'll sign the agreement and you'll never see me again." My desperate bargaining brought faint smiles to their faces, since they thought I was coasting on my family name and had no real business experience. Worst of all, I was a girl, and girls don't run distilleries. At least, not in their eyes.

Three days wasn't a lot of time, but I'd either save the company that I loved, lived and breathed, or I'd sign the fucking papers and hand everything over to the jackals around this table. Something inside of me rebelled at the thought of my company in the hands of these men. They'd sell it off piece by piece, starting with the copper stills.

Holloway studied my face carefully, then laid his hand on my shoulder as he made his recommendation. "I say we give Selena three days. As hard as she's worked to keep the distillery afloat after her dad's death, we owe her that."

From the way their faces fell, you'd have thought I was

asking for the moon, not one last chance. At least there was one good thing about the board—they always listened to their lawyer.

"All in favor?" Holloway's lined face relaxed slightly as the board members reluctantly lifted their hands, surety written in their faces that I would fail at this, just like I'd failed at bringing the company back from the edge of bankruptcy.

I didn't care about their derision. They were just a bunch of old men who wanted to continue feeding off my family's hard work like a bunch of starving lampreys. I didn't care how much I had to debase myself. I didn't care if I had to lie. I would save this company, and I'd do it by defying my father's number one rule:

No matter what happens, Selena, don't you ever contact Bastian Forge.

Yeah, contacting a two-hundred-year-old vampire was probably risky, but choosing between my life and my family business... I'd do *anything* to save this company that had been in my family for over two hundred years.

Because without it, I'd be nothing.

Langston-Forge had been in my family since 1771, and we still did business in the same building in downtown Philadelphia that we did in those early days. My office was the same one my great-grandfather occupied, and I'd always felt the sense of history—*and responsibility*—of that bond especially deeply.

Deeper than my brother, who signed a five-million-dollar promissory note with a local loan shark and then had the nerve to die before he paid it back. Which wouldn't have been the worst thing ever, except he took my dad down with him. Asshole.

Leaving me in charge of a multimillion-dollar distillery that was struggling, even though we were the oldest one operating in the United States. We'd beaten Prohibition, rising costs and increased competition and survived. But nothing, it seemed, would survive my brother's mistake. I spun in my chair, my gaze landing on the dusty painting hanging on the brick wall, conveniently spotlighted by new LED lighting.

I strode to the picture and blew away the dust clouding

the air. The artist had depicted a cruel-looking man of about thirty with a classically sculpted face, shadowed eyes and dark, swept-back hair. Added together, the effect was mesmerizing—falling somewhere between classically beautiful and smolderingly sexy.

To me, he was neither of those things. For me, Forge only represented hope.

I'd stared at that painting for longer than I cared to admit, especially since I'd taken over the company. I'd been toying with finding Forge and asking for a loan for months now, and every single time I considered it, my emotions warred between intrigue and fear. According to family legend, Bastian Forge's reputation had always fallen somewhere between a savior and a devil, with emphasis on the latter.

Truthfully, I knew little about him except for cautionary tales. But every generation of Langstons knew the family secret, then passed it down to the next. We'd founded our company on a generous loan from a reclusive vampire, which was why his name still appeared on the company stationery, as well as the front of the building.

Still, it was easy to forget he existed.

No one had seen him in the flesh, not since our ancestor took the money and signed the agreement, which hung right next to the painting. The penned accord had almost faded away, but the signatures were still clearly legible—Adolphus Langston and Bastian Forge—in a dark, aggressive scrawl that I knew was blood.

"I can't believe you still have those relics hanging up. I told your father to put them in storage a long time ago." Holloway's voice still carried a touch of Southern honey, even after all this time in the north.

I shrugged as I turned to him. "Family tradition, I guess."

Emerson Holloway, Esquire, was the only person I trusted these days, and to that end, I didn't mince words. "I'm going to find him and ask him to bail out the company." I didn't add the word *again*, even though I was thinking it. "That's why I asked for three days."

His already pale face went sheet white. "Selena, you know..."

"Yeah, I know." I waved my hand around, but only managed to stir up the dust still hanging in the stagnant air. "He's dangerous, we swore an oath, he's impossible to find, blah, blah, blah."

Part of the original deal was that no Langston, however desperate, was to ever seek him out. But the company going under and being sold off piecemeal was definitely worse than desperate. This was end-of-the-world shit. Besides, he probably wasn't even alive anymore, so this was most likely a total waste of time.

Except...someone had left a note on my desk two weeks ago.

It was signed Bastian Forge, in the same angry scrawl as the agreement.

The security cameras came up blank, as if he'd materialized in and out.

"Selena." Holloway's voice took on that gentle, let-me-talk-some-sense-into-you tone that I'd grown so fond of over these past six months. "Maybe it's time to let this place go. After what your brother did, I don't think we can bounce back from that. I've done everything I can think to do to save this place. I'm sorry."

He wasn't lying. Holloway had dedicated his life to this company, and my family. The inside joke was that our blood flowed eighty proof, unless we were having a bad day, and then it flowed a hundred and fifty, and nobody had better light a match.

Unfortunately, my brother never believed in family, or blood, or loyalty. His passions leaned more toward cocaine and gambling, hence the sketchy multimillion-dollar loan. When Dad tried to help Brandon out of his situation, they'd both ended up dead in a car at the bottom of the Delaware River, each with a single shot to the head. I'd never forgive Brandon for that, never forgive him for allowing Dad to get caught up in his troubles.

By the time the police had wrapped up their investigation, I was running the company and didn't have the luxury of grieving. But I could still hold on to my anger.

After Dad—who was also our master distiller—died, distributors stopped ordering. They were worried about quality control and delivery issues, and I didn't blame them for doubting. Who was going to trust a twenty-year-old with no apparent business sense to run a respected company?

"I'm going to save Langston-Forge, Emerson. Any way I can." I didn't know if Bastian Forge was still alive—the note not withstanding—but if anyone knew where he was, it would be Holloway.

"Contacting Bastian Forge is not the way to save *anything*. You can rebuild…"

"Twelve years, Emerson. That's how long it will take to rebuild from scratch." *And in the meantime, my whisky—the best I've ever made—will be bottled and sold by someone else. Or, worse yet, thrown into a blend where no one will ever taste it.*

"You're young, Selena. Twelve years is not that long."

"We only need enough operating capital for six months," I countered evenly, watching his lined face for a sign he'd help me instead of talking me out of this.

Holloway took off his glasses and rubbed his eyes, leaving them red. He'd put hours into negotiating this deal, from petitioning the bank for more time, to maneuvering the board to make me a handsome buyout offer. I didn't want the money. I wanted to run a world-class whisky distillery. All I needed was a chance.

Holloway's face seemed haggard as he said, "You sure have a lot of faith in those barrels in Warehouse Seven."

"Yes. I do."

Warehouse Seven held eight thousand barrels of my father's last batch of whisky. We fondly called it the platinum batch, and in six months we could bottle and distribute it. I'd been a kid when I helped Dad mix this batch twelve years ago, and it had aged well. If I could hold on to the company for six more months, our worries would be over.

"We have over fifty million dollars in that warehouse, Emerson," I insisted. "I'll see it distributed under the Langston name."

"And Forge," Emerson reminded me wryly. "Don't forget him."

"Trust me, I'm not." I wasn't used to asking for favors, so it took me a moment to spit it out. "I wasn't kidding about what I said. Tell me how to contact Bastian Forge. I'm asking him for a short-term loan."

"I don't—"

"Before Dad died, he said you knew where he was." I was bluffing, but Emerson didn't know that. He only knew that I'd been at Dad's side ever since I was little, especially after his stroke. It was a plausible enough explanation that he'd told me this secret.

Of course, I left out the part where Dad warned me to never try to find Forge, since I figured that would only give Emerson more ammunition to deny any knowledge of the vampire's existence.

"I'll go to the bank and negotiate another extension. I have a few favors I can call in," Emerson said, his voice soothing.

Sorry, Emerson, we're way beyond that now. We need cash.

"You'd be wasting your time. How do I contact him?" I said, sensing his reluctance. After six months, he should know how stubborn I was. "I won't be put off. Forge is our only chance to save the company." I scanned his exhausted face. "You know what the board will do. They'll sell this place off and Langston Forge will be forgotten. We could be a great company, Emerson, one of the best in the world. You know it and I know it. We only have to hang on for six more months."

Emerson searched my face and, apparently, saw I was telling the truth. Also, he knew I'd just badger him until I got what I wanted. "I'll have to find the letter. It's in the safe somewhere. I've never even opened the envelope."

Joy tugged at my heart before I told it not to get too excited.

The mysterious note had only contained one line, other than the signature, and I sincerely hoped he meant what he said.

Find me if you need my help. Bastian Forge.

That sentence—his offer of help when I was drowning —had been echoing in my head for weeks. And now he was my last hope.

"Do it." My eyes strayed back to the painting. "I want this resolved, one way or another, before my three days are up."

3

Six hours later, I stood in front of a pair of intimidating gates and debated my sanity.

"He left me a note," I reminded myself softly. "He practically asked me to come."

As it turned out, Forge wasn't that hard to find, once I had his address. And Google.

Now all I needed was a shot of liquid courage and I'd be good to go.

As tempted as I was to sneak a sip from the bottle of whisky in my sweaty hand, I refrained, reminding myself of how stories were born. Bastian Forge might be painted as the devil, but like with any good story, every one of my ancestors had probably exaggerated Forge's threat. Multiply that by ten generations, and the man took on the aura of an evil monster.

"Ridiculous. He's just a guy who loaned my ancestor money," I told myself. "Once he tastes this, he'll be all in. I know it."

The bottle clutched in my hand held a distilling of Dad's final batch. Six months early, yet...the whisky was outstanding. It was the perfect balance of smoke and burn, a touch of citrus and a bit of spice. I'd never tasted anything like it, and after all that had gone wrong in my life, this was the one thing I knew was right.

This whisky would propel L&F to the top.

Besides, I reasoned, all I was asking for was a short-term loan. Surely the vampire wouldn't refuse to save his own company, preserve his good name and cement Langston-Forge's reputation as one of the world's finest purveyors of small-batch whisky. I couldn't see a downside for him.

However, I also didn't see a way inside these imposing gates.

A faint buzzing to the left drew my attention, as did the red, blinking light on the speaker box that hung by two wires from its mount. "Leave the delivery at the gates. Thank you."

I didn't see a button to push, so I leaned in. "I'm here to see Bastian Forge." I brandished the bottle in front of the derelict speaker, as if they could somehow see it.

"Name?"

"Selena Langston. Tell Mr. Forge I've come bearing gifts."

The best thing about whisky was nobody ever turned it down, and when the gates creaked open, as if they hadn't moved in years, I stepped through, positive my plan was off to a good start.

One last lingering look at my ten-year-old Civic, and I started up the overgrown driveway. Older-than-dirt trees bent over the driveway, casting long shadows across the weed-filled gravel drive. When the house came into view, though, my steps faltered.

"Holy shit."

The house—*monstrosity*—that rose before me out of a

small grove of saplings could be the setting for every scary vampire movie ever. It was a Gothic mix of grey stone covered in ivy with a steeply pitched roofline and dark, arched windows. The building's wings stretched out to my right and left, as far as I could see. The dilapidated garage was missing a door, and inside, a lone mid-century car languished on flat tires.

Was I really any smarter than any of those idiots in every horror movie ever?

Stubbornness pushed me forward another few steps, until my feet faltered in front of the tall door with peeling black paint. Before I could talk myself out of this foolishness, I rapped hard, as if daring him to ignore me.

It shouldn't have surprised me when the thing swung open and nobody was behind it except for an inky, unfathomable darkness. The place smelled empty, of dust and closed-up rooms and food gone bad. The scent was strong enough to be overwhelming. I could have just turned around right then. I could have marched back to my shitty little car and signed the papers and started over, just like Holloway suggested.

But deep inside, a light glowed yellow, so I stepped inside and shut the door behind me. I could barely make out the form of an imposing man as he emerged from the lit doorway, then the shadows swallowed him up before I got a good look. His buttery-smooth voice floated down the hall to me as he murmured, "Selena Langston."

"That's me." Internally I winced at my flippant tone, but I kept my back straight. I was a Langston, damn it, and I had nothing to be embarrassed about. It wasn't my fault the company was drowning in debt, and if I could just convince this guy to...

I sensed him approaching through the shadows, but I

couldn't see anything in the darkness. For a breathless few seconds, he was nothing but an ominous shadow gliding silently toward me, and then Bastian Forge stepped into the light. That was the moment I realized I was completely in over my head.

At first glance, he was everything my family had warned me about, and then some.

I didn't have much experience with vampires, but he was enormous. Tall and rangy, he stalked toward me, making the spacious entry seem claustrophobic as he filled it up with a pair of broad shoulders and a bad attitude. I deduced this by the half-snarl curling his lip—and his eyes. I couldn't see the color, but I swear to God, they glowed. My heart stuttering, I couldn't have run if I wanted to.

There was no doubt it was Forge.

Every line of his handsome face—the one I'd stared at longer than I should have—was exactly like the old painting. But unlike in the artwork, his high, sharp cheekbones and sweep of black hair were accented by an aura of careless arrogance. He filled the air with power—it seeped from him like a drug, intoxicating and frighteningly seductive, and despite my best efforts, it affected me. But it wasn't his size or intensity that had me reevaluating my sanity; it was his cold, impassive tone.

"Miss Langston. I assume you were warned against contacting me? Which means you are not only reckless, you are incapable of following orders."

I was neither of those things—*mostly not*—and bristled at his accusation.

"I'm perfectly capable of following *orders*, as you call them, but not when my company is on the line."

His skin was paler than I'd imagined, so the painting

wasn't one hundred percent accurate. Or he'd spent the last few centuries indoors.

"Nevertheless, your ancestor swore an oath to me," he said. "I expect that promise to be honored."

"That was two hundred years ago. Surely there's a time limit for honoring an agreement?" I plowed ahead, fueled mostly by fear and desperation, because maybe, if I got the words out fast enough, somehow, he might actually listen. "I'm losing the company. It's about to revert to the board of directors, who will dismantle it and sell it off to the highest bidder. Langston-Forge is all I've got." I raised the bottle so the amber liquid caught the light. "Except for this. Once I decant this batch in six months, L&F will be liquid again. Literally. All I'm asking for is a short-term loan."

"Get out of my house."

I bit my lip, probably a no-no when in present company, but I couldn't help myself. "Please. I don't have anyone else to go to."

Menace flashed across his face before he schooled it into a calm, detached mask. "They don't have banks these days?" Hostility emanated from him, filling up the hallway, making the hair on the back of my neck stand up. This was not a vampire to be trifled with, but I was looking at my very last hope. God, I wish he wasn't so pissed off.

"But...what about the note? You left me a note offering your help." My brain seemed to have slowed down.

"I don't know what you are talking about, but let us assume that concludes your business here." He took another step toward me, and this close, I had to look up to see his eyes. The hostility in them was nothing short of frightening.

My lungs contracted in fear as I debated my options. *None.* I had no options. This was it.

"No, it doesn't conclude anything," I said. The hand holding the bottle was slippery with sweat. I hoped I didn't drop it on his floor. "I found a note on my desk. Signed by you." My brain grabbed on to bits of information like they were life rafts. "You contacted me *first*. Aren't you interested in saving the company you founded?"

"Not in the least."

His answer threw me for a second before I recovered. "Why not?"

He frowned down at me, his eyes narrowing. "Because I was never interested in the business, not like your ancestor. Ambrose took my money and built his company, and the only thing I asked for in return was to never be bothered. *You are bothering me.*"

"Fine." I shoved the bottle forward. "Taste this and tell me it's not the best you've ever had. If it isn't, then I'll go away."

For a second, we stared at each other, then his top lip inched up, revealing a glint of a fang.

Infernal humans. It's a wonder they've survived this long.

That was *Forge's* grumpy voice, *in my head*. I looked around, convinced I was losing my mind.

Incapable of following simple instructions.

That was definitely Forge speaking, even though his lips hadn't moved and he was still staring at me like I was a fly he wanted to swat. His voice rang in my head, and not like a reverberation or an echo. It was as if he was speaking directly into my consciousness.

It's no wonder I've never found one I liked half as much as Ambrose.

I snorted. "I might be an infernal human, but I'm also a Langston—just like Ambrose. I'll save my own damn company and take your name off the building, you pompous asshole." I drew a deep breath, trying to come up with a pithy parting shot. "I don't need...your help."

Not exactly the scathing jab I'd been going for. I cradled the bottle so it didn't slip from my hands. "Like I said before, I'm perfectly capable of following instructions. *When they make sense.*"

Whirling, I made for the door, the whisky safe and my temper on fire. No way I'd waste anything this good on Forge and his glowing-eye freak show. But when I tugged on the knob, the door didn't budge. "Open the damn door," I growled over my shoulder at him. "Open it or I swear..." I yanked the handle again while balancing the precious bottle.

I wasn't even scared, which really said something about my self-preservation instincts, but damn was I mad. Before I could get out another word, Forge appeared beside me.

"You heard my thoughts?"

"If you mean the freaky insult thing you just did inside my head, then yes, I heard you, loud and clear. I hate to tell you this, but you aren't a huge prize either, hiding in the shadows in your enormous house." I kept my hand on the knob. "Let me out."

Ambrose came to me with a proposition. How much did I loan him?

"A thousand pounds sterling," I snapped, and his face changed, ever so slightly. "Happy? Can I go home now?"

Impossible.

"Weird, but clearly not impossible." My mind was spinning. *I could read vampire thoughts.* Over twenty years and this had never happened to me before. Of course, I'd never been this close to a vampire before, either. I would have pondered this further, except I had to *get out of this damn house.*

"I'll help you."

"Too late. I don't want your damn help. Not after hearing your opinion of me." Dad would say I was just cutting off my nose to spite my face, and maybe I was. But damn it, after months of trying to fix Brandon's fuck-up, after losing Dad, after trying to earn the board's respect—and failing—I was tired of defending myself to men. Vampires, I decided, were even worse.

"I will provide you enough working capital to last you six months and pay off all outstanding debts."

My hand fell away from the door as I weighed his generous offer. I was still pretty pissed off, though. "That's a lot of money. I can't pay you back until—"

"I don't want your money," he said abruptly, the eerie glow sparking in his eyes. "All I want in return is a favor." He went still as I considered my answer. So still that I was tempted to poke him to see if he was still alive.

I eyed him suspiciously. "What kind of favor?" He didn't look quite as frightening anymore, but there was something in his tone that made me hesitate. "I think I'd rather repay the loan."

"I have a very delicate meeting to attend in a few weeks, and I have a lot riding on the outcome. If I knew what my adversaries were thinking, it would give me an edge in the negotiations. Accompany me, and I'll forgive your debt entirely."

"Nothing is ever that simple," I said. "What's the catch?"

"It's called Assembly—a meeting of the high vampires in my clan." He cocked his head, as if sizing me up for dinner. "I can't read their minds." This time when he smiled, I got the full-fang treatment. "But you can."

4

_____

As I waited for her to respond to my offer, it struck me that the girl was the spitting image of her ancestor, right down to her curly blond hair and slanted emerald eyes. For the first time in a long time, I felt a twinge of...*curiosity* toward a human.

Whatever desperation had brought her here, it was her gutsy determination that convinced me she might be of use to me—if her ability was real. Once I determined that, I'd still have to train her, which I wasn't holding out hope for. She couldn't be more than twenty, and I briefly wondered why she was shouldering this burden by herself.

Selena tossed her hair over her shoulder and turned her eyes on me. She was suspicious, but there was a kernel of hope growing in her gaze. "Where is this meeting?"

"Scotland." The same place I'd met her ancestor, but I saw no need to mention that. Not until she agreed. Even if she did...

"Why do you need to know what everyone else is thinking?"

I almost laughed. "Obviously, you haven't sat through many negotiations."

"Enough to know that reading people's thoughts is like..."

As she floundered for the correct word, I helpfully supplied it. "Dishonest?"

"Exactly."

"Nonetheless, will you help me?" Her thoughts were everywhere, fluctuating between dismay and optimism as she weighed my offer against her fears. Watching her internal debate was fascinating, and when she chewed her bottom lip—when those white teeth closed over her pink lip —my cock twitched against my pants. *Well, well—that's a surprise.*

"When is this mysterious meeting?" She was clutching that bottle like a lifeline, so I took a step closer, noting she didn't shrink back, although her heart rate sped up. I held my hand out for the bottle, and she obligingly slid it into my palm, the glass warm from where she'd been holding it.

"Let me explain everything, then you can decide. In the meantime, tell me about this." I gestured to the bottle.

"It's a special blend. This"—her face brightened as I held the bottle up to the light—"will transform Langston-Forge." She had a breathy way of speaking when she was nervous, and her scent was musky, tinged with sweetness. She was exquisite.

"A bold claim," I said evenly. Her ancestor had said much the same, and while Langston-Forge was a respectable enough distillery, its product was hardly groundbreaking. American whisky was still just whisky. I should know.

"Do you even drink whisky?" She licked her kips, and again, I closely followed the flick of that pink tongue before

I pulled my attention away. "Or do you drink...you know...*blood*?"

"I happen to enjoy both." Seeing her slight wince, I added, "But whisky will do for now." I motioned her to follow and flicked the lights on in the kitchen. "Let me get two glasses."

After setting them out, I let her do the pouring, and her hand stayed steady, despite the misgivings she must have. But desperation gave people courage, and right now, Selena Langston would take on an entire army to save her company. I wasn't an army, but I meant to take advantage of her desperation, as well as her ability. While she fussed with the liquor, making sure both glasses were filled evenly, I sized her up.

She was small and willowy, but her stance was confident, and her jaw was set in stubbornness, much the same way as Ambrose. Pale blond hair flowed down to the middle of her back, and she had a faint dusting of freckles on her nose. A bonny lass, I might have called her once. Now, as lovely as she was, Selena was just a means to an end.

"Cheers," she murmured as our glasses touched, then she raised it to her lips and swallowed, closing her eyes in bliss. Her throat was a long, pale column, her lashes lay dark against slightly flushed cheeks, and then there was that wild tumble of silky hair. Just looking at it made me want to tangle my hands in it, see if it was as soft as it looked.

I wiped all lascivious thoughts from my head—in case she could hear them—and sniffed the whisky. A vampire's smell is so acute that we can pick out individual ingredients, processes and age with the barest inhalation. This particular combination was divine—rich, but subtle, with only a hint of human-world smells.

The second the whisky hit my palate, I knew her claim was correct.

I'd never tasted anything like it, not even in Scotland. It was the perfect blend. The woody balance was superb, the burn exquisite, and where some whiskys were overbearingly fruity, this one was not. No, this flavor was more complex, deeper. It reminded me of long ago, when everything was still done by hand. I tasted a hint of peat, which was a surprise, given we were far from Scotland.

"What do you think?"

I'd been completely lost for a moment. I looked down at my empty glass. "It's...indescribable."

"Good. That's what I needed to hear." She set her glass on the counter and braced her hands on the edge. "When is this meeting?"

Straight back to business, which I had to admire. "Two weeks." I tipped another three fingers into my glass, then savored my next taste, perhaps even more than the first. "But before you agree, know that you will need some coaching."

"I suppose you'll be the one doing the coaching?" Her tone—a mix of sass and arrogance—made my cock jump again. Obviously, isolation took its toll, since I was attracted to the first female I'd seen. Seeing how this might get complicated, I almost withdrew my proposal, but much like Miss Langston, my options were short.

I poured her another glass as well. "Only if you wish to succeed at eavesdropping," I said slowly, feeling out her reservations. Interestingly, she didn't seem scared—she seemed intrigued.

"Given that I'm only doing this—not that I actually am —at your request, it's hardly eavesdropping. It's more like spying."

"Exactly," I agreed, grateful that she saw the difference. "You don't want the others to suspect you."

"What? Or I'll get eaten up?" All I saw were laughing eyes over the rim of crystal. At some point, when I didn't answer, realization dawned on her face. She shook her head. "Oh, no way. Why can't I just repay the loan?"

"Because your ability to read a vampire's mind is more valuable than any currency," I explained patiently. "Now that I know what you can do, I don't want your money. I want you at that meeting." With her by my side, I'd discover why the Elder had summoned me to this ridiculous meeting, especially seeing the crimes were so very old.

But this could actually work. Formal Assembly was held so seldom that there were always new faces amongst my old clan. *And* there was precedent for my offer to train Selena. A reason no one at the meeting would question. A reason that could be easily explained.

As part of the Ouroboros Society, it was my duty to protect humans with special abilities or gifts. Despite all my time on Earth, I'd never had the opportunity to exercise my membership benefits. While I'd never expected to find one waiting on my doorstep, I would certainly use this situation to my advantage. Even if she was descended from the only human I'd ever considered a friend.

"Let's say I actually agree to do this...thing. The loan will be considered repaid, and you won't expect me to do anything else for you?"

Considering how hard my cock was right now, I debated answering her honestly. She was lovely, but I'd sworn off humans years ago and had no intention of pursuing this one. *Especially* since she was the descendant of my only human friend.

Instead, I lifted my glass to her. "Once you bottle this,

you won't need me—or anyone else—to save your company." It was said to stoke her confidence, but with good whisky still burning in my mouth, it was hardly a lie.

When she clinked the rim of her glass against mine, the sound rang through the empty house.

"*Our* company."

5

Forge's reaction when he tasted the whisky made me feel oddly vindicated. He was hard to read, but from the expression on his face, he really liked it. Given how old he was, I figured he had a refined palate. Besides, there had been a second, right as we toasted, that made me feel like we really were partners, and not just names on the company letterhead.

"All right, I'll do it." After mentally tallying my reservations, I listed them off one by one. "No breaking the law, not even a bit. No messing with anyone's mind, because that would be like malpractice or something. And only this one meeting, nothing else, ever." Just the thought of looking into someone else's thoughts creeped me out, but again, saving the company was high on my priority list.

"Agreed." We'd moved to the kitchen table, and he leaned back and crossed his legs, looking all refined. I might have believed it, too, if not for the instantaneous nudge inside my head. His smile grew wide as the nudge turned into a weird scratching on the inside of my skull.

"You should know vampires can read human

thoughts effortlessly," he said. "As you can hear my thoughts, they will be able to hear yours." His expression didn't change as he added, "Which means you have very little time to learn how to protect yourself from the likes of me."

I tried pushing the scratchy feeling away, but it turned insistent, growing stronger until my left eye twitched. Reflexively, I shoved harder, scared I couldn't exorcise the sensation out of my very own head. *Is this what a nervous breakdown feels like?* I wondered.

"That's me, trying to get into your head. I'm about to read your thoughts, every single one, in explicit detail." He took another slow sip of whisky. "Pushing won't get rid of me. I'll just find another way around."

"Stop it, Forge."

"Make me, Selena." The pompous bastard sounded like he was enjoying this.

The insistent, grating sensation in my skull was making me panic. "Fine. Then explain how I keep you out of my head." A horrifying thought occurred to me. "You'd better not be looking around while you're in there, because that's just rude."

I took his smug smile as a definite yes. Pissed off, I shoved against him even harder, my knuckles turning white as I gripped the edge of the table.

"Instead of pushing, try surrounding yourself with an impenetrable barrier, like a shield."

What he was suggesting was so foreign that all I could do was stare. "I can't build a shield out of thoughts. That's impossible."

"Yes, you can. Like this."

A cool sensation replaced the scratchy one. With it came a quiet I hadn't known in months, since before my life turned into a shitshow. It felt wonderful to turn off the world, if only for a moment.

This is how you do it.

I still don't understand.

Watch me, Selena. Watch what I do.

I followed him as he created a temporary shield, blanketing my thoughts with a seamless, secure barrier that shut out all outside noise. I felt second-rate as he effortlessly wove together an invisible, yet soothing coat, then, just as quickly, made it disappear.

"Now, copy what I did. Imagine yourself surrounded by layers of mental shields. A wall that no one can breach, and only you can allow someone access."

"Sounds good," I said, trying to recreate the complexity of what I'd just seen. I couldn't even wrap my head around it, much less figure out how to begin. "But it still makes no sense."

"Then close your eyes, Selena, and watch me as I show you again." This time his shield felt like a warm blanket, soft and comforting, before it solidified into something concrete. Impenetrable. I tentatively touched the smooth shell, noting the patterns in it, the intricacies. Still, I laughed when Forge said, "Now. Use mine as a template and create your own."

It took forever, but I tried to copy Forge's shield the best I could, my structure nowhere as complex. Clumsy, almost. But I didn't stop until I was done, my efforts resulting in a sloppy, lopsided replica of his.

"Okay, there, my shield is up." I grinned, fueled by competition and maybe a bit of liquid courage. "I'm ready. Bring it on."

With a smile, he ripped mine away.

"That's not fair," I protested. "I worked hard on that."

"It was more like a leaky ship than an impenetrable

safe," he said, ruefully shaking his head. "Poorest first attempt I've ever seen in my life." But there was something in his face, a trace of emotion that might have been humor.

Was he messing with me?

"I don't think it was that bad." I added, "How long did you say I had?"

"Two weeks, Selena. But that's enough for today. There's always tomorrow to practice."

I couldn't leave before I wiped away that condescending note in his voice. "Again," I demanded quietly. "Show me again." This was how I'd learned the whisky business, after all. Nagging Dad until he showed me everything. Then learning whatever I could from everyone else at the plant. Sure, my knowledge base was haphazard, but I'd learned from the best. I just hoped Forge knew what he was doing.

The look that crossed his face—was it surprise or doubt? —was accompanied by a shake of his head. "Enough for today. You can return tomorrow evening for another lesson."

"Again, or the deal's off." Somehow just knowing there was an entire race of beings who could read my thoughts whenever they wanted to disturbed me. I figured I'd do everything I could to protect myself. Plus, I had a willing teacher, as long as I did his dirty work.

Again, Forge's cool, soothing shield encompassed me, and this time, I was more thorough in my exploration, then slowly replicated it. Definitely not perfect, but definitely better. When I was finished, I waited for Forge to tear through it.

"Very good, Selena. You're a quick study."

Warmth blossomed inside of me, perhaps a bit hotter than it should have. It had been a long time since anyone had noticed my efforts, much less praised me for them.

"I thought you said—"

"I will transfer five million into the company account tomorrow morning, via Mr. Holloway. Will that amount be sufficient?"

I blinked, trying to fathom the obscene number he'd thrown out so nonchalantly. "I don't need that much, honestly. Just enough to hold off the creditors until this batch is ready."

"Five million," Forge repeated, pouring me another finger of whisky.

"Two million," I countered.

"Five," he said, then held up a hand when I went to protest. "You really are bad at negotiations. No one bargains for *less money*." He lifted his glass, then took a long draw. This time, I drank in the way his face changed as the whisky rolled down his throat. It made him look almost handsome.

God, what if he heard me? Panicked, I double-checked my shield, finding it intact. I hoped.

"Yes," I said. "That amount works for me."

"Then we have a deal, Miss Langston."

His hand, when he pulled me up from my chair, was cool, but his grip was firm as we shook on it. I slogged down the dark, eerie drive and to my waiting car. I spent the rest of the ride home wondering if I'd just sold my soul to the proverbial devil.

6

The next morning, Emerson Holloway was waiting for me in the lobby of the Langston and Forge offices. Before I got within ten feet of him, I knew he was spoiling for a fight, and I knew why.

"What did you do, Selena?"

"What I had to. I take it the money has already been transferred?"

Emerson ignored me completely. "Five million. What did you promise him?"

"Repayment," I replied, relief making my stomach do flip-flops. For the next six months, I was free of the ever-present anxiety I'd learned to live with. They couldn't repo the building, or the product, and the board couldn't break up the company. All I had to do was finalize my plans for the release in six months, and watch my hard work pay off. I felt so light that I thought I could fly.

"Pay the grain vendors first. They've been waiting the longest. Then go down the line, oldest invoices to newest. I don't want them waiting another day longer than they already have."

"Give Bastian Forge back the money, Selena," Emerson urged, his arms crossed across his chest, his shirt rumpled. He'd spent the night here again, probably searching for a different solution. Anything other than taking money from a vampire. "Don't accept it."

We'd been meeting payroll, but barely, and I was sure the employees knew it. "Give everyone a bonus. I'll leave the amounts up to you."

"Please, Selena, listen to reason."

"I don't want anyone worried about their job, nor the stability of this company."

"Fine. But I'm warning you, you'll regret taking the money."

He might be right. In fact, doubt curdled in my stomach along with the sushi I'd had for lunch, but did I really have a choice? I decided no, we didn't, and by the end of the day, all our debts had been settled. Well, all except for my debt to Forge.

"I know you think I'm making a mistake," I told Emerson as I paused in the doorway of his office on my way out. "And maybe I have. But you can't tell me this company isn't worth saving."

Beneath the lights, he looked exhausted. "It's worth saving, but not like this."

"I did the only thing I could do, and it will all work out." I smiled at the man who'd helped me through these hellish months. "Go home and get some rest. We can all sleep better knowing everyone is paid and happy. Besides"—I grinned at him—"I have a new batch to start, and I have some wild ideas."

An hour later, I pulled up in front of Forge's. I'd told him I'd come by for another lesson in mind protection that didn't involve a tin-foil hat, although I had to admit, I was having some misgivings.

Did human laws even apply to vampires? Wasn't this a little like wiretapping? Or was it something worse?

This time, the gates were thrown wide open, and light glowed from every window, giving me a better idea of the size of the place. Even in the dimming light, I saw that the brush had been cut away from the drive, and the ivy seemed to have disappeared from the stone walls of the mansion.

I knocked and then went through when Forge called. Or I heard *something* from inside the house, although I couldn't be sure it was Forge's voice. *Let's pretend it was an invitation.*

As I wandered through the house—where was he?— every room was alight. Glittering crystals dripped from ornate chandeliers, oils hung from every wall and the dark wood gleamed. It even smelled like someone lived here; the air was filled with the scent of lemon and cedar. I didn't detect a hint of damp and dust.

"Selena, I'm so glad you came." His deep voice came from behind me, and I forced myself not to turn around. *Nope, I don't need to see if his hair is still glossy and thick.*

"Yeah, well, can't have vampires prying inside my head now, can we?" I joked.

"We certainly cannot."

I stepped into the room, a cozy space with a couple of chairs and a huge round table with an arrangement that towered over me. Some sort of small waiting area. Forge nodded to one of the chairs.

I didn't even have my coat off when the sensation hit me, and this time, it felt more like maggots squirming than scratching. I floundered around with my arms caught in my sleeves, hastily erecting my barrier. It ended up a disaster— a half-built orb full of ragged holes. Forge had the nerve to laugh, and even though I knew it wasn't my best work, it wasn't fair. He hadn't given me any notice.

When I tried again, he only laughed harder.

"Fine," I said through gritted teeth. "What about this?"

I'd been practicing all day, as a matter of fact. Work had taken a back seat to the idea that my thoughts were accessible to vampires, and I'd been at it so long that my brain felt like mush. I held my breath until my lungs hurt, then pushed.

My barrier snapped into place, and whether it was fueled by anger or desperation, somehow, I managed to erect something that might actually keep him out.

"Now that's more like it. Just like Ambrose, you're a natural."

7

I hadn't intended to laugh at Selena.

But I couldn't stop.

My mirth wasn't directed at her, but at her sheer stubbornness to keep me out of her head. Well, maybe at her getting stuck in her coat. I'd obviously angered her, but as she stood before me, her hair tumbling over her shoulders, flames practically coming out of her nose, she took my breath away.

Fuck, she reminded me of Ambrose, her far-off ancestor —pissed because I didn't understand his single-minded dream for his precious whisky. We'd spent more than a few nights at odds with each other, but I'd respected his tenacity. He'd had a short temper, just like her.

As well as an uncanny ability to know what someone was thinking.

He didn't have Selena's gift—was nowhere near as perceptive—but Ambrose had enough intuition that he always seemed to know what was on someone's mind. He was right enough times that I came to rely on his opinion. Of course, Ambrose and I were human back then. Just two

Scotsmen bonding over something as simple as whisky. While our lives took different paths, our abiding friendship had survived.

Even after I was changed.

Even after my interest in the human world waned, and my involvement with my new race prevailed. When I made costly errors that brought me to America, Ambrose had followed. Once again, it was the two of us in a strange world, and when Ambrose asked me for a favor—the only thing he'd ever requested—I gave it to him.

But the past wasn't my concern—it was the enraged hellcat in front of me, hair spilling down over her shoulders and fire sparking in her eyes. I gave her a minute to ready herself, waiting until a cocky smile curved her lips.

"Try getting through this, Forge."

God, she was something else, challenging me to rip through her mind, positive that she could withstand me. Just the fact that she called me only by my last name—a sign of disrespect, even contempt, in my world—made me laugh again. No one else would dare. No one but her.

Her eyes narrowed to mere slits, she was so pissed off.

"Are you ready?" I asked, muting my humor. I doubted she'd stay if I laughed one more time.

In answer, she jutted out her jaw and set her hands on her hips.

I was gentle—not that any of my brethren would be— and touched her shield, running an invisible finger down along it. Goosebumps exploded on her arms, so I did it again, enjoying the way her skin pebbled.

Even though we stood ten feet apart.

"Forge..." Her voice wavered slightly, and I got a hold of myself. Fuck, what was I doing? She would perform this favor, and then we'd part ways. Humans were liabilities, and then they were dead, so there was no use getting close to them. They didn't last long enough.

Something I'd convinced myself of two lifetimes ago, and was doubly sure of now.

"Forge?"

"I'm going to tear through your shield, Selena. I won't hurt you, but note where I indicate weak points, then shore them up. Strengthen any thin areas and patch up any holes. They will look for those, and if they find them, they will be merciless."

She could have argued, but she nodded instead. Reaching around, she pulled her hair back, revealing her huge eyes and perfect skin. Not that Selena knew she was beautiful. No, her whole focus was to keep me out of her head, so she could save her company. Keep her word and honor our agreement.

Except the longer I was around her, the less I wanted that debt settled.

It had been a long time since I'd noticed beauty of any kind. But knowing she'd be returning tonight, I'd made some efforts to spruce up the house, a fact that pissed me off. I wasn't used to changing anything in my life for a stranger. Especially not a human stranger. Yet...I'd done just that.

Nor could I help myself from running my fingers over her shield, enjoying the small, almost unnoticeable shiver that went through her. God, she was intriguing.

"This is very good work, Selena." True, her shield wasn't perfect, but it would keep most vampires out of her head. Quite a feat after only a day. "You've been practicing."

"I did. You said two weeks, but I have business dealings to take care of, and deliveries to check, so I wanted to get this out of the way."

I shook my head. "This is more important than work. If you go with me to Scotland, you have to be able to protect yourself."

"Nothing is more important than the company. Speaking of which, how long will we be gone? I can't be away for more than a day or two."

I respected her commitment to the company, but I hadn't been lying—she had to protect herself; otherwise, the others would know exactly why I'd brought her to the meeting. If they did, they'd discover why she was there, and it would only be me standing between twenty vampires and her.

"Assembly is Saturday evening. Factoring in travel time, we will be gone three days."

In truth, I only planned to be in Scotland long enough to attend the meeting. From takeoff to landing back in Philly—I figured no more than fourteen hours, total. Long enough to figure out who wanted me dead and shove their antiquated laws back down their throats. But now, thinking of spending three days alone with Selena...

"I can't do three entire days," she protested, her cheeks flushing as she fumed. Her shield was falling apart.

"Really? Five million dollars, and you can't spare three days?"

I figured a little guilt was better than a full-blown argument. I had learned *something* about women in all my time on this planet.

Selena's face betrayed her every thought as she went to war with herself. I didn't even have to read her mind—her face gave her away completely, something else we'd have to conquer before I'd allow her around any of my kind.

"Fine," she said reluctantly. "Three days." She didn't look

happy about it, but that was one less hurdle. This way we could...

I shook the image out of my head. What was I hoping for? That we enjoyed the trip? That I'd tumble into her bed, and then what? After only two days, I was attached, and I couldn't afford to be. I had to remember that Selena was a tool—*my* tool—to survive Assembly.

"You have to be ready," I warned her, pulling my mind away from the consequences if she failed. "Which means we keep working on this. As for your temper...you must learn to control it."

"I can do this."

"I know you think you can. But I'm not putting you in a dangerous situation unless you're prepared." *Since when?* I asked myself. She was useful to me, that was all. But even telling myself that, I knew it was a lie. My membership in the Ouroboros Society came with only one requirement— protecting humans with rare abilities—and right now, that edict was at odds with my objective, to survive Assembly.

Safeguarding humans didn't exactly mesh with using her ability to give me an edge with my brethren, but damned if I wouldn't try to do both. I'd never met—never heard—of a human who could read vampire minds. But now that I had, I felt the urge to protect Selena, even as I trained her to spy for me.

"I'll be ready," she insisted. "I don't even know why...but I'm inclined to help you." The sweet scent of fear mixed with adrenaline filled the space around us, and I drew a subtle breath. It went straight to my head, and I turned away as my fangs descended. She leaned forward in her chair. "Besides, I'm not in the habit of letting anyone down."

That much was apparent. She was smart and deter- mined, but she was so damn young that I couldn't fathom how she'd ended up in charge at Langston-Forge. Yet when I'd skimmed through the company website, there she was, front and center as the acting CEO.

Pretending I was inspecting the flowers, I asked, "How did you end up running the company? You're a bit young for that much responsibility."

"Just for future reference, those are the kinds of questions you get in trouble for asking these days." When I turned, she raked me with the same derisive look I'd given her when I first saw her. "It wasn't like I asked for it. I was in college, taking business classes, hoping that maybe, someday, I could step into Dad's shoes at the distillery."

Her face flushed, and even from here, I heard her heartbeat speed up. "But then my asshole brother decided to clear all his drug and gambling debts by putting the company up as collateral. It took everything we had to pay off the loan shark. Since then, it's been a constant game of catch-up."

As before, myriad emotions flickered over her face. Regret, anger, resignation.

"This brother of yours, where is he now?" I knew my voice had turned hard, but I couldn't help it. If I were her, I'd wring the little shit's neck and force him to repay the damn loan himself. I couldn't imagine being so irresponsible to risk everything my family had built for a personal debt.

"Dead, along with Dad."

Fuck. I'd assumed she was a spoiled-rotten rich girl the first time I saw her. But that wasn't it at all. She was fighting to fix her brother's screwups and fill her dad's shoes, with all her hopes riding on some barrels in an old barn.

While I was using her to leverage a situation to my advantage.

"You are saying none of this—the company, the loan from me—none of this was your doing?"

"Not really. But Langston-Forge has employees who depend on us, a reputation to preserve and someone had to step up. And I'm the only Langston left."

8

A s I gave Forge the short, no-frills version of the last six months of my life, his face changed, ever so slightly. Granted, I'd only known him for a day, but if I didn't know any better, I'd say Forge was angry.

"Look, it's no big deal." I waved it off. "Sure, I'd planned on finishing college first, but it isn't like I'm a noob or anything. I've spent more time at L&F than anyone except maybe Holloway. You could say I've picked up a few things along the way."

"Who mixed the special batch you brought yesterday? You know, the bribe to maneuver me into helping you?"

Now I smiled, glad that Forge saw it for what it was. "That was Dad's last batch, from twelve years ago. He believed it would be special, swore up and down this would put us on the map. But he had a stroke later that year and was never the same again. He couldn't use his left side, and his memory... It was pretty bad after that. But I helped him mix that day, and I took careful notes. I've used that same recipe ever since."

Forge grew more intense, if that was even possible. "How much more do you have?"

"Eight years' worth. Almost one hundred and fifty million dollars, if I've calculated it correctly." Regret and anger ached in my chest while I added, "But this batch? When I bottle this one, I'm naming it after Dad."

Forge didn't say anything about that, but I got the feeling he approved. "This man, you called him a loan shark? What about him?"

"He made some noise at first." *Like threatening to kill me.* "Hoping to squeeze more money out of me...or rather, the company. But he left us alone once he discovered how close we were to bankruptcy." A small laugh escaped my lips. "Can't squeeze blood from a turnip, Dad always said."

"His name?"

"It's over, Forge. Leave it alone," I warned him. The expression on his face got darker, deep furrows forming on his forehead. He wasn't scary, exactly, since I didn't think his anger was directed at me, but my breathing picked up when our eyes locked. I seldom lost a battle of wills, but it was me who dropped my gaze first.

When I looked up, he was right in front of me. I'd never even seen him move.

"It's never over with those people," he growled, offering me an up-close view of his fangs. Viscerally, I was shocked at the sight of them, my muscles freezing, although I wasn't sure what I'd expected. Forge was a vampire; I knew that. It was only that he *seemed* so genteel, while nothing about those long, sharp canines was civilized.

"It is, I promise. He's gone."

For a second, I thought he'd ask for the loan shark's name again, but he must have decided against it. His eyes were completely unreadable when he ordered me, "Go home. Keep practicing. I'll see you tomorrow."

This time, I followed his orders without question.

9

—————

Ten minutes later, I was navigating the winding roads back to the city, replaying Forge's rather abrupt brush-off. I thought maybe he'd give cracking my shield another try, but we'd veered into territory that—especially in my dark car on a dark country road —I deeply regretted entering.

I hadn't intended to go to him, hat in hand, begging for money, then lay the clusterfuck that was my life right in front of him. Far from it. I intended to secure the loan, pay him back in six months and never see him again. A one-and-done sort of thing.

I'd saved the company, but now circumstances were throwing us together too often for comfort. The bigger problem was that there was something about Forge that made me want to tell him everything. *He probably thinks I'm crazy.* I groaned, maneuvering the car around a tight turn.

I wasn't even lying when I'd said I wanted to help him. For some reason—maybe simply to avoid my own problems —I was looking forward to this Scotland trip, even if it did involve vampires. I'd always planned to go, but life got in the way, more times than I cared to count.

Besides, I was beyond curious about this freaky ability of mine. I didn't understand it, but with Forge willing to help me, at least I had a safety net. A grumpy, enigmatic safety net, but still, I had someone to help me through this. While I was grateful, questions continued to stack up. Could it be genetic? Some kind of family curse, although I'd never heard so much as a whisper of such?

Or was it a fluke, with no rhyme nor reason to it?

I mulled over that one for a few miles, chewing on the possibilities. The human world and the vampire one rarely —if ever—overlapped. It wasn't like I knew much about them, despite Forge's historical entanglements with my family.

If vampires were a mystery, then Forge was the biggest one of all. I'd been fascinated with Forge my entire life, from the mysterious loan, to how he'd gotten tangled up with Ambrose in the first place. He was the skeleton in the Langston closet, and I always assumed everyone had one just like it. It wasn't until I was fifteen that I realized not every family personally knew a vampire, much less put their name on the front of the building.

Stories about Forge—and about Ambrose, my whisky-loving ancestor—were traded between Dad and Grandpa, between Holloway and Dad, between the long-timers who'd worked for L&F their whole lives. I'd listened to every single one, some more than once. The result? I was completely mesmerized by Bastian Forge, which was why I'd left his painting up. Just a little reminder of the family secret, and the vampire who'd become somewhat of an obsession.

I didn't hear from Forge for a week, which was strange, considering our deadline.

When he did contact me, it wasn't with a scrawled note thrown on my desk. He sent me a text message. Brutal and to the point, which I was learning was Forge's style.

We are ready to resume. Come prepared.

———

THAT NIGHT, the gates were once again thrown open, and the gardens looked almost sculpted as compared to a week ago. Like last time, light blazed from the windows. And, like then, Forge ambushed me, just before I managed to extricate myself from the car. I ended up getting caught in the door this time, and tumbled out onto the gravel.

"You need to learn to always be prepared, Selena," Forge said as he offered me his hand. I ignored it and dusted gravel off my ass.

"Every second of my life?" I asked. I'd agreed to help him with this distasteful favor, but I had demands at the company, decisions to make now that we were in the black again. When I'd approached Forge, I didn't think I'd be worrying about mind-reading vampires. Come to think of it, how was I supposed to tell the difference between vampires and humans? Forge looked... Well, true, he looked different than any human I'd ever even seen before, but maybe that was an anomaly. Surely all vampires weren't this muscled and hot.

Shit, Selena, mind reading—remember?

He observed me carefully, his face going blank when he saw how closely I was watching him. "Of course not. You have to be able to protect yourself, and that means being prepared. You know what happened last time; you should have expected me to try something similar tonight."

"Yeah, well..." I'd spent the entire drive here mulling

over the puzzle that Forge presented. Instead of, like he'd said, *readying my defense*. "Okay, point taken. Try again."

This time I actually managed to hold him off for almost a minute. Then my shield cracked like an egg and split open, offering up my innermost thoughts like an oyster. "No mind reading," I warned him sternly.

"I wouldn't dream of it," he assured me as he ushered me inside. The house seemed...newer, somehow, as if twenty years had been taken off the interior. Each room was polished and sparkling, now that they weren't languishing in the shadows. Unfortunately, I only got a glimpse of each, because with Forge leading the way, I practically had to run to keep up. He was dressed in a black V-neck sweater and matching slacks, but instead of making him look urbane, the combination made him look danger-ous. Sexy.

"This is...gorgeous," I commented as we passed by yet another opulent room. "How long have you lived here?"

"I built this place around nineteen hundred. I've been here since, though I do still own a property or two in Scotland."

God, I wished he'd slow down a bit. I hustled to keep up.

"Do you go there often?" It seemed like a perfectly innocuous question, but his face darkened, and I kept my mouth shut after that. No sense in stirring anything up. I wasn't looking to know his most intimate secrets, just making polite conversation. At least, that was what I told myself as I sized Forge up from behind, most definitely *not* looking at his spectacular ass.

Previously I hadn't had an opportunity to study him, since I was usually trying to keep him out of my head. He was an imposing figure. He walked with the careless ease of a powerful man, and as we turned down another hallway, I wondered how big this place was. Certainly bigger than it looked from outside.

"I thought that tonight we'd practice in here."

The dark hallway opened up to a greenhouse, the domed glass roof offering a fractured glimpse of the stars and a dark blue velvet sky. The space was empty, just a barren flagstone floor and glass all around us. The lack of walls gave me the feeling we were floating in nothingness. I'd never been afraid of the dark, but the hair on the back of my neck stood up as I scanned the impenetrable woods outside.

"You've made progress, but you still have far to go. Tonight, we'll make that shield of yours impenetrable. Ready?"

I'd barely nodded when he was in my head, working to break my shield apart. I scrambled around, patching holes, fixing cracks and generally putting out fires as he poked holes in my hard-won barrier. "Come on, Forge, give me a break here," I pleaded as he once again stripped away another section, leaving me exposed.

A smile edged up one side of his mouth when I called him Forge, but he didn't stop, and by the time we took a break an hour later, I had sweat dripping down my back and my head was spinning. "Okay," I said, certain I had the hang of it this time. "How about this?"

This time when he poked, my shield held. It might not be completely impenetrable, but it was definitely my best work so far. When he flashed me a smile—little more than an upturned corner of his mouth—I held my breath and got ready. Although I felt that unnerving maggot-squirming sensation, he wasn't able to rip through it.

"That, I believe, will do, Selena."

A feeling of euphoria filled me up, both from knowing

I'd mastered this, and because of the pride in his voice. Even though it was ridiculous, I thrived on success and, apparently, having someone tell me so.

"That deserves a drink, don't you think?" he said.

I did think so. Relief caused me to lower my guard, and without a word, Forge ripped away my shield. *Bastard.*

This time there was no doubt that Forge smiled, his white teeth flashing in the dark.

"I'm no bastard, just for the record." His soft laughter filled up the greenhouse. "Always, Selena, your shield has to remain in place. Especially during the meeting—no exceptions. If anything goes wrong, you will protect yourself, and not worry about anything else."

"Well, okay." I grudgingly settled my shield back into place and trudged behind him as he led the way back through the bewildering maze of rooms. He flicked a switch and a chandelier blazed to life and illuminated the room. We'd ended up in a library. A gorgeous, beautiful library.

"Wow. Now this is a room I could spend hours in." I did another turn, slower this time, taking in the dark, carved bookcases, the obvious expense of the rugs, the huge chandelier in the room. And the books it contained. With shelf after shelf of gold-embossed covers, I'd never seen anything like it. My hands itched to tip one out and take a closer look.

"Anytime you'd like," Forge commented absently as he set two crystal glasses on the huge desk. "You can help yourself, so long as you return them. There are some I'm quite fond of."

I reached up and stroked a spine. The leather felt papery, soft almost, and up close, they smelled delicious, like fall leaves. I pulled the book closer, squinting—*Charles Dickens, A Tale of Two Cities.* It was probably a first edition and worth a fortune. I gently pushed the book back in with its neighbors.

"For now, I'd like your opinion on this," Forge said as he poured two healthy fingers into the glasses from a crystal decanter. Which meant I had no way of telling what this actually was. When he handed me the glass, challenge shone in his dark eyes.

"Nice color," I commented, holding it up to the light. Not quite as pale as my whiskeys, this had more of a chestnut color, and the smell... I drew in the heady scent of caramel and toffee. "What is this?" I wondered out loud as Forge sank into one of the leather chairs. The smell was...intoxicating, almost nutty, but I still smelled the oak underlying the peaty aroma.

"Taste it and tell me—you're the expert," Forge said, raising his glass to his lips, as I did the same.

God, it was like sipping heaven. Forget Dad's special batch; this was deeper, richer, so many layers of flavors, and damn if I couldn't help but take another sip. "It's... I've never tasted anything quite like it," I told Forge. "*Never*, and I've tasted pretty much everything on the market, since keeping up with our competition is a necessity."

His smile turned secretive, a challenge I couldn't ignore.

"It's old," I offered haltingly, trying to put the exquisite taste—*the experience*—into words and failing miserably. "Older than anything I've ever tasted, maybe." Age was the only explanation for the depth of the flavor. A crazy idea occurred to me, though I immediately discounted it.

As if he knew my thoughts, Forge's smile grew wide. Forget handsome—set against the elegance of this room, he became every bit as beautiful as his surroundings. I, on the other hand, was most definitely out of place.

"When was this made?"

"When do you think?" he asked, the overhead light glinting in eyes that seemed to be laughing at me. For a second, I got caught on how his dark hair complemented his pale skin, then I shook myself.

"It can't be what I think it is." When he did nothing but watch me over the rim of his glass, I guessed the impossible: "This is Ambrose's whisky."

"The woman knows her whisky," he said, his face frustratingly unreadable as he lifted his glass to me. "Unfortunately, I only have this bottle left. I decided it was time I open it. *Sláinte*."

This time, when we clinked our glasses together, we both smiled.

"There is one more thing to take care of before we leave for Scotland," Forge said, setting down his glass and leaning forward, elbows on his knees. "Your face is like an open book. Other vampires won't have to read your mind, not when they can read your face so easily. We have to work on your poker face. If you can master that, then you'll accompany me. Otherwise..."

My heart sank.

When, exactly, I'd decided that I really, really wanted to go to Scotland, I didn't know, but I wanted it desperately. I wanted to be part of this Assembly, whatever it was. I wanted to stretch my wings, see what I could do. "All right. But what does it matter what anyone else thinks about me?" From everything I knew about vampires—which, granted, was mostly from reading steamy romances—vampires hardly even cared about humans. In fact, I was banking on the fact they'd just ignore me completely.

"They'll be curious about you, at the very least. While it's not unusual for clan members to bring a companion to Assembly, they will be suspicious of you. I would tell them you're my lawyer..." A corner of his mouth twitched back up. "But we don't use lawyers." His humor faded away, leaving that serious, inscrutable look on his face. "Assembly lasts for one hour. During that time, your face must be as impenetrable as your mind." He sighed. "Right now, you're worried you won't be going to Scotland at all. If I can read you that easily, then my brethren can as well."

"Okay, well... I've never played poker, and I'm used to speaking my mind. What do you suggest?" I'd never had to control my emotions, for God's sake, and given my admittedly bad temper sometimes got away from me, this newest task might prove more difficult than building my shield.

Forge pointed to a mirror hanging between two bookcases. "Face the mirror and watch how your face changes. Then figure out how to create a mask that no one else can read."

I faced the mirror, and the only thing I noticed was how tangled my hair was. I wished I'd taken a few minutes to spruce myself up before I arrived. But no matter; Forge didn't care about anything except that I could see into other vampires' minds. "Okay, I'm ready."

"If you don't go to Scotland, I expect the money to be paid back."

My mouth fell open before I had the sense to snap it shut. "But you said—"

"Look at your face, Selena," he said gently. "You can't show them every last thing you're thinking. Let's try that again."

This time when he said it, I forced my face to remain smooth, settled into an expression of disinterest. It felt like my cheeks had rigor mortis, and my eye was beginning to twitch, but from the approval on Forge's face, I knew I was on the right track.

"That's much better. You have five days to get *that* expression down perfectly, and we can leave. If you can't convince me you're ready, then you stay behind."

During the pause, I sensed he wanted to add something else to that, but instead, he said, "Practice as often as you can. Be here on Friday at seven o'clock. Not a minute before." He seemed to put extra emphasis on that last word, but I was thinking about the money, and not keeping up my part of the deal.

"And the loan?" I took the last drink of my whisky, still amazed that it was Ambrose's.

"We made a deal, Selena." A smile quirked his mouth. "I know you won't let me down."

10

Friday, otherwise known as the day of *my final test that I hoped I passed*, came faster than I'd expected. True, I'd been practicing the face thing in the mirror, but nothing, it seemed, ever fully prepared me for Forge. Which was why I locked my shield into place before I even passed through the gates.

I arrived an hour early, planning—for once—to ambush Forge before he ambushed me, and I was feeling pretty damn smug, positive I'd get the jump on him as I parked the car and crept silently up the front steps.

"Now we'll see who wins *this* round."

The house was darker than usual, only a few lights on, and I pushed the door open after my faint knock went unanswered. True, I wanted to sneak up on Forge, but it still didn't seem like a good idea to just let myself inside a vampire's house. Much like the first time I was here, the rooms were dark, but after a quick pass through the first floor, I didn't find Forge anywhere.

"He's probably waiting until I get close, then he'll jump out of the shadows and make me pee my pants," I muttered, starting to get annoyed. I knew he was here somewhere, because the hair on my nape prickled occasionally, as if someone was watching me.

If Forge thought he could just pop out from some dark corner and I'd be able to keep a straight face, he was wrong, because the longer I wandered through the empty house, the more freaked out I became. Seriously, who did this sort of thing? It was almost cruel.

By the time I'd made my second pass with no sign of him, I figured Forge could just find me. I headed to the library, or to where I remembered the library being. Because my sense of direction is shit, I ended up back at the greenhouse that wasn't really a greenhouse at all, more of an empty snow globe. Tonight, the moon was rising just over the top of the tree line.

The slight prickling at the base of my neck returned, and was the only thing that prepared me for what came next. About the time I realized I wasn't alone, a vampire forced their way inside my head. For what it was worth, my shield stayed in place as the squirmy feeling wiggled through my brain. I slapped a hand to my forehead to stave off the no-holds-barred aggression behind the incursion.

"Jeez, Forge. Enough already. That hurts."

Thankfully, I remembered to school my face into something other than a grimace of pain before I turned around. If Forge saw anything on my face except a blank mask, I'd never make it to Scotland.

The vampire filling up the doorway was indistinct, a misty form that was more a collection of shadows than an actual physical being. A low, malevolent chuckle issued from the center of the dark shadow, which was most definitely *not* Forge.

As the trespasser wormed his way further inside my head, I fought back, bracing my defenses like they were my only hope of survival. In response, the pain intensified, knives raking over my skull until I was sure that my brain was being eaten away by little white squiggly things. While my face remained perfectly blank, I was very much afraid, and fear instilled me with enough strength to keep this intruder out.

"Who the hell are you?" I managed, trying to mask the tremor in my words.

"Look at the little human. You're able to keep me out of your head. Has Bastian been giving you lessons?" Just the tone of his voice told me I was in terrible trouble. It was clinically curious, but at the same time, completely devoid of humanity. "Do you belong to him, girl?"

I don't belong to anyone, you creeper, I wanted to say, but the words got jumbled up in my throat by terror.

I blinked, and he'd cut the distance between us in half. While I didn't want him this close to me, I got a better look at him. His coloring was light, and not just his smooth, pallid skin. Where Forge's darkness contrasted with his skin, this vampire was completely devoid of color; his hair was almost white, while his nearly colorless eyes seemed to swallow the moonlight.

"Where is Forge?" I demanded, realizing too late that if this creature was inside the house, with no Forge in sight, I was in some serious shit. "Again, who the hell are you and why are you in this house?"

"Disrespectful little human," the vampire growled, gliding further into the greenhouse, as if he didn't have actual feet. Totally unnerving effect, and one I hoped to never experience again. Between scrambling to shield my precious brain from his painful incursion, and my entire body freezing in fear, I was pretty sure these would be my final breaths.

He'd almost reached me when Forge's deep voice cut through the silence. "Do not take another step, Dobson."

"Forge. Thank God," I muttered, half pissed at him. Of course this was a setup—I should have expected him to pull something like this. What I hated even more was the impulse to throw my arms around him in gratitude. "For your information, this was a really stupid test."

"This isn't part of the test, Selena. Do not move a muscle."

Indeed, neither me nor the strange vampire had moved since Forge appeared. Me, because I'd been pretty certain I was about to become dinner. Watching the stranger's face, it was apparent that was what he was thinking about, since he eyed me like a side of beef, licking his grey-tinted lips.

"If you take one more step, Dobson, I'll rip your head off and leave you outside for the sun to turn to dust." Forge's voice was thrumming with violence as he took a step closer to the two of us.

Not a test. Forge's warning finally registered. This vampire was not part of the test, and given how he was looking at me... A ripple of fear shivered through me, and Dobson refocused with preternatural intent.

"You have two seconds to dematerialize. If you aren't gone, we'll do this the hard way," Forge said, his voice booming in the enclosed space. Dobson hissed like he was an actual snake, which sounded so wrong coming out of his mouth.

Right before my eyes, the person—vampire—disappeared into thin air, leaving me alone with Forge, my mouth hanging open once again. I snapped it shut, pissed that I'd probably blown my chance at Scotland.

I was so busy looking at the empty spot where Dobson had disappeared that I barely felt Forge touch my shoulder. "Selena, are you all right?" he asked, and for once, I *could* read his face—it was taut with anger, but lurking in his eyes was something that looked like concern. When his hand closed around my arm, I realized how badly I was shaking.

"I... Yeah, I think so. I'm not..." Shit, now that the threat was gone, my body was going through some kind of adrenaline-fueled reaction, as my stomach cramped up and the shaking grew steadily worse.

"Did he get into my head?" I demanded angrily as Forge led me from the greenhouse. "Can you tell?" I was in a full-on panic, just thinking how that...*thing*...had access to my thoughts. "Why was there someone else here tonight? Is he a friend of yours?"

It occurred to me that I had no right to question Forge's friend circle, but damn, it was beginning to dawn on me just how close a call this had been. What would have happened if Dobson had reached me? I had no doubt I'd be lying on that cold floor, my throat ripped out.

"No, not a friend. Not even close." Forge paused, looking into my eyes intently, and I felt him run invisible fingers over my barrier, still locked firmly into place. "No, your shield appears to be intact."

Forge's voice held the same relief that I felt down to my bones. *Thank God.* The thought of someone like that inside my head—and the damage they could do—turned my stomach.

"If he's not a friend, then why was he here?"

"Summoning me to Assembly." Forge didn't sound at all happy about it—not the meeting, nor the person who was just here. "You're early. I gave you a specific time to arrive, and I expected you to honor that." From his sharp, clipped tone, I realized he was angry, really angry, and that threw me, since emotion was such a departure from his usual unflappable demeanor.

"I *am* early. I just thought..."

"You didn't think. You were so focused on beating me at my own game that you disregarded the rules." His dark eyes turned glacially cold, his voice like a knife as he continued, "None of this is a game, Selena, no matter how much you pretend otherwise."

"I've never pretended this is a game. It's you who changed the rules, by setting moving targets for me to hit. Not that I haven't hit every single one," I added, just so he didn't forget I'd successfully kept him out of my head.

"Have you really?" he drawled, as if he sensed—or heard—my self-satisfied jab. In an instant I was stripped bare as he tore my shield away in one fell swoop. The pain from being suddenly exposed felt like a bright light stabbing straight into my eye.

"*That's* what Dobson could have done to you. Left you exposed and vulnerable. He could have made you slit your own throat, or walk off a roof. He could have killed you before you even knew he'd moved, or drunk you until there wasn't a drop of blood left in your body. *That's* how much danger you were in, just because you couldn't follow the rules."

"You asshole," I hissed, my hands balling into fists. He'd started this, he was the one dictating the rules, setting my next hurdle to jump. He was the judge I had to please in order to even make it to Assembly. Whatever in the hell *that* was.

As his face tightened up, I knew I'd gone too far.

"No, I'm not an asshole, Selena. I'm much, much worse

than that. And it's about time you found out just how much more."

His eyes grew so dark that even the overhead lights didn't penetrate his rage. The planes of his usually handsome face turned hard and unforgiving under the bulb's faint glow. Shadows crawled beneath his skin, like bruises looking for a place to land, and my heart lurched as he glided toward me.

I realized that over the past week, I'd lost whatever sense of caution I had first exercised around Forge. Somehow, I'd not only become comfortable with the notion of being around a vampire—I'd actually grown to look forward to our time together. Just like complacency was a bad idea in the distillery business, complacency around a two-hundred-year-old vampire could have deadly consequences.

But there were two things Forge didn't count on. I was a Langston, and Langstons didn't back down. I was also a woman, and stubbornness ran in my blood. Add the two together and I turned into a brick wall that was every bit as impenetrable as he was.

"I'm not afraid of you, Forge," I said, with false courage. "You knew I was coming here tonight. An hour shouldn't mean the difference between life and death."

He closed his eyes for a second, as if praying for patience —*do vampires even pray?*—and when he opened them, some of the ice had disappeared.

"Rules are put into place for a reason. But obeying them seems to be an issue with you. If I hadn't sensed your distress when I did, he could have really hurt you, Selena."

"And here I thought you didn't care, Forge."

"Oh, I care. Especially now that I've been officially summoned by the clan. Now I don't have a choice. Dobson saw you, so you're going. Whether you're ready. Or not."

"I'm ready. He didn't get through, even though he tried." A terrible thought occurred to me. "But you got right through. Have you always been able to bypass my shield? Have you been playing with me this whole time?"

He seemed to debate it for a minute. "Just because *I* can doesn't mean anyone else can. Your shield will keep all but the strongest vampires out. You face, however..."

"Yeah, I know I need to work on that."

"Keep working on it. We leave tomorrow morning. I'll have a car pick you up."

"A...car? Like a car with a driver?"

"Ah, I'm impressed," he said wryly. "Yes, Selena, my car with a driver will pick you up at nine o'clock sharp. Please be ready when he arrives—the flight leaves at ten."

"And you were going to tell me this...when?"

"After you passed the final test, which, as we know, you failed miserably. However, we will have time to practice on the plane."

"It's going to look weird, us making faces at each other on a plane. What do you think the passengers will think?"

"The only passengers on the plane will be you and I, Selena," Forge said, ushering me toward the door, his tone completely sarcastic. "Do you really think I'd fly commercial?"

11

As it turned out, there were things I really liked about Forge's life. Being ferried around in a big, fancy car was the bomb, but when we reached his plane, my mouth dropped open. I'd seen private jets like this on TV, but never in real life. I climbed the steps to the sleek plane, hoping we'd have really good snacks for the flight.

Normally I hated flying, but excitement pooled in my stomach at the prospect of traveling on such a luxurious aircraft *and* landing in Scotland. I didn't know where in Scotland we were going, but I was sure there would be a distillery within a mile of us, and I planned to visit one. Or more, if we had time.

Forge was in one of the soft-looking leather seats, staring out the window. I didn't think he'd even noticed I'd arrived, his dark coloring in stark contrast to the plane's creamy interior.

It hadn't really hit me until then that I was flying to a strange country with a strange man to do something I'd never done before. I hadn't exactly taken the time to plan any of this out. A tinge of hesitation rippled through me, and that was the moment Forge turned his head, and we locked eyes.

There was a hint of concern in his, as well as pleasure when he saw me, his lips curving upward.

That was it. I knew I was on the right track. Bastian Forge had been part of my family—and therefore, my world —for my entire life. Something in me relaxed as he smiled, and I felt no undercurrent of regret or doubt, only anticipation of what was to come. I might not know a lot about my ability, but I had Forge, and we were going to Scotland. For now, that was enough.

"Pick a seat, Selena."

I chose the one opposite him, set down my bag and searched for the buckle. I'd never been on a private plane before, and couldn't find either end.

"Right here." He reached around me, his hand brushing my neck. "Can't have anything happening to you now, can we?" he whispered in my ear as he clicked the belt tight.

"Not until I get to see Scotland," I quipped, the side of my neck burning, even though his touch was cool. Before he noticed the blush in my cheeks, I turned and looked out the window. Then I was pressed back into the seat as the plane took off, Forge barely shifting as we rocketed into the clouds.

THE MOMENT SELENA ducked into the Bombardier 7000, my heart loosened up. I hadn't been entirely sure she'd come today, not after last night. If I hadn't gotten there when I did...

I kept my eyes turned to the window, watching the car pull away. I'd replayed last night a million times, debating whether I should have killed that bastard on sight. Which would only have made this war between me and the other vampires attending Assembly more dangerous.

But Dobson had gotten within ten feet of her.

Ten fucking feet.

That was what I was thinking about when I felt the shiver of hesitation—of doubt—that went through her as she halted in the aisle, uncertain, her hair pulled back so all I saw was those huge green eyes.

When I caught her gaze with mine, a smile creased her lips, lighting up her face, and whatever bound up my heart loosened slightly. I was happy to see her. I was glad she was going with me, even when I knew how high the stakes were.

As hard as I'd fought my attraction, I couldn't get her out of my head. Whether it was her strange ability, her stubbornness or how intriguing I found her, I didn't know. But for the past two weeks, Selena was all I'd thought of.

A savage thrill went through me at the combination of awe and pleasure that crossed her face as she surveyed the inside of the plane, before she remembered to school her expression into a serene mask. As I watched her lock down her emotions, disappointment welled up. I hated that this task required her to learn how to hide her feelings. I much preferred reading her like a book. Vampires were an aloof, dispassionate race, and after years of playing mind games with my fellow bloodsuckers, I hadn't realized how much I'd missed seeing actual emotion on someone's face.

She looked up and down the plane, taking in the sophisticated interior. "Pick a seat, Selena." After a small hesitation, she sat right in front of me, set her bag aside, then occupied herself looking for the belt.

"Right here." When I reached around to pull the belt into place, I let my hand brush her cheek, the first time I'd touched her since the handshake that set us on this path.

Her skin was velvety, so warm that the heat penetrated my fingers. She was so nervous that I wondered if she'd ever flown before. "Can't have anything happening to you now, can we?" I told her, my lips almost touching her ear.

In true Selena form, she responded, "Not until I get to see Scotland."

We were already rolling down the runway, although I doubted Selena even noticed, she was so intent on measuring up the interior of the plane. When the pilot took off, she gripped the arms until her knuckles turned white.

"Selena," I said. She turned her head, and I glimpsed fear in her eyes before she managed to shutter her emotions away. "We'll level out in a minute and this feeling will pass. Haven't you ever flown before?"

"Yes, and I forgot how much I hated it." Her face turned whiter. "I thought, when I saw this fancy plane, that the takeoff would be easier for me to handle." Her voice was breathy. "Don't hate me if I get sick all over your beautiful interior."

"Look at me." She immediately obeyed, stubbornness forgotten, and I let my face soften, my muscles fighting me every step of the way. She blinked in surprise when my hand covered hers and I felt the bones beneath her soft skin. "Haven't you ever been to Scotland?"

"No. Dad always said he'd take us, but then he had the stroke, and things changed."

"That's when you started helping him?"

"Yeah. Brandon never cared about the distillery, except to use it as a piggy bank. Which meant Dad relied on me, more and more, as time went by. In the end, I was at the distillery more than I was home. When I realized I'd be the one to take Dad's place, I went to college, since I figured business classes would come in handy. I made it through two years before Brandon screwed everything up." She squeezed her eyes shut. "Then it was all on me..."

I doubted she even knew what she was saying, but talking would get her through takeoff, so I listened as she went on about her shit brother, her father, the company. *Unfair.* Humans always whine about how unfair life is, but in Selena's case, it was true. She'd been dealt a shit hand and was doing her best to get through.

I'd already decided—if I survived Assembly—that Selena would be my first priority when we returned. She was unique in every way, and I intended to see just how far her abilities went. I'd make sure the loan shark never bothered her again, and in the process, I'd find out what had really happened to her brother and father. The way everything fell on her shoulders—she thought it was just a series of bad luck.

I saw things differently, and I planned to do something about it.

"You got awfully quiet over there, Forge. Am I that boring?"

"Not at all. I was just thinking. I'd say between your hands-on experience and your classes, you're more than prepared to handle the company. Langston-Forge is lucky to have you."

Her face bloomed even pinker, and she turned away again, thinking I hadn't noticed. If she thought I wouldn't notice the flush of blood in her skin, she was sorely mistaken. Her scent was so ingrained in me now that I couldn't ignore the truth any longer.

I wanted her. I had no right wanting a human, much less Selena Langston, but I did.

"You don't even know me, Forge. You have no idea if I'm competent or not."

Except she was completely wrong. Over the last seven days, I'd made it my goal in life to research every aspect of Langston-Forge, from their profit and loss statements, down to their last employee. The company had limped along for the past six years on loans and extensions, and that was before she'd had to cash out everything to pay off the loan shark.

"Besides, I've hardly done a bang-up job. Without your money, everything would have reverted to the board. They planned to liquidate the company and sell if off piecemeal to any interested parties. I don't know about you, but I couldn't just sit by and watch it happen, not without trying *everything*."

In the end, her reckless plan to come and ask me for a loan had worked.

"How did you convince Holloway to give you my address?"

Her mouth quirked upward. "Isn't it obvious? I didn't take no for an answer." Her eyes grew serious. "He warned me against you, and rightfully so. Nobody's seen you in forever."

Exactly as I'd planned. "What did you think, that first night?"

"Arrogant," she said, without missing a beat. "But fair, I suppose. At least you listened to me, and gave me a chance."

Not exactly a glowing report, but then again, as reclusive as I was, it was on point. When I'd pressed the button and opened the gates to let her in, I'd been motivated by curiosity. Her curly hair had been a dead giveaway, and it had amused me that the Langstons had finally broken their oath.

Then she'd walked through my door.

Now she was sitting in my plane, and I was taking her to

a gathering of my old clan-mates. Reaching out, I had her other hand in mine before I even knew I'd moved. Her skin was warm, a reminder that she was human, and what she about to walk into would be like a foreign world to her.

"You can still back out of this."

I wasn't sure why I was giving her an out this late in the game. Especially when everything rode on the outcome of this meeting. Who the hell was I kidding? I'd rather navigate the deadly intricacies of Assembly myself than put Selena in any danger.

It was a mistake asking her to do this, to involve her in the mess I'd made. My life was on the line. No reason to risk hers too. I was just opening my mouth to tell her that when she cut me off.

"I don't want to back out." She shot me a blinding smile while she squeezed my hand, hard. "I mean it. I really want to do this. Not just because of the loan, either." She shrugged. "I'm curious about my ability. I'd like to see what I can do, I suppose."

"How much do you know about me?" *About us?*

"Just..." Her eyes searched my face. "Are you sure you want to hear this? I mean, you've become kind of a legend in my family, and I don't want to offend you."

When she turned her face to the window, I waited her out until she finally started talking again.

"I know you were friends with Ambrose, and that you loaned him the money for the company, no questions asked. I know you never wanted your name on the distillery, but he did it out of gratitude. When you became a vampire, the two of you remained friends until he died. And none of us were to ever try to contact you."

"Like I said before, obedience is not your strong suit."

Her smile turned defiant and she rolled her eyes. "I had

a damn good reason to find you. Besides, my approach worked."

"What else did you hear?" I didn't particularly care, but I wanted to keep her talking, at least until the plane leveled out and she released her death grip on my hands.

"Not much. Most of the stories I've heard...can't be true. They have to be exaggerations." Her gaze skimmed my face, then shifted away. Clearly, I should be more interested in the Langstons' stories.

"What else did you hear about me, Selena?"

"You once killed another vampire to save Ambrose. After that, Ambrose tried to cut off all contact with you, but you insisted on keeping him in your life. You were once the most powerful man—*vampire*—in Philadelphia. Once you even dueled with the governor of Pennsylvania, and after that you disappeared. The next time anyone from my family saw you was at Ambrose's funeral, and you warned his son to never contact you, but your name could remain on the building."

So, a mix of fact and fiction. There was no duel with the governor, and I hated my name on the building. It surprised me that Ambrose had said anything about the night I killed one of my kind to save him, but then again, my friend was always full of surprises.

"Mostly true. All except my name on the building. I never intended to be part of Langston company's operations. Not then, and not now." Emotions played across her face— confusion and surprise. "But I'm glad it's still there, because otherwise, you would have never come looking for me."

"It wasn't..." A strange look came over her face. "There was a note, Forge. Someone left me a note, with your signature. That's why I came looking for you."

"You told me that the first night." I'd forgotten, but now

that she'd brought it up, a flicker of misgiving went through me. "Out of curiosity, what did it say?"

"'Find me if you need my help.'" Her grip relaxed slightly as she pulled back to scan my face. "It was signed by you—the signature was exactly the same."

"How do you know what my signature looks like?" I asked, wondering who might be playing games. My friendship with Ambrose was ancient history, and given I'd been in virtual hiding for centuries, there was no one looking for me. Except, of course, the Elder. But involving humans in vampire affairs was now only frowned upon, it was foolish. And the Elder was not foolish.

"I just... *I know*, okay?" She pulled her hands from mine and turned to hide her blush. I was tempted to peek into her head to see how, exactly, she knew, but that would be a terrible betrayal, and not one I was willing to make.

Selena didn't noticed the plane had reached cruising altitude until I leaned over and unbuckled her belt. "It's a six-hour flight to Edinburgh. Make yourself comfortable— there are drinks over on the bar."

She went over and put her hands on her hips as she surveyed the assorted bottles. "You brought Dad's bottle."

"I thought it might bring us a bit of good luck," I told her, although the real reason was something I couldn't admit, not even to myself. "There's ice just below the glasses."

When she returned, she handed me a glass, then clinked hers against mine. "Do you always toast when you drink?" I asked, thinking this was perhaps a new tradition.

"No, only with you. But it seems like we are always either celebrating something or one of us is trying to cut a deal."

"*Sláinte mhath.*"

"Slang-var what?"

"*Sláinte mhath*," I said again. "Good health in Gaelic, if you will." I watched her mouth the words over and over again between sips. She had the most inviting mouth, and if I didn't stop thinking like that, I was going to get both of us killed.

"I like the way it feels on my tongue. It's almost like drinking good whisky, isn't it, speaking Gaelic?"

I decided I could watch her drink whisky all day, from the way her throat moved as she swallowed, to the slight flush of pink in her cheeks.

"I've never thought of it that way. As a matter of fact, it's been a long time since I've spoken that language." Once, it had been the only language I'd known. Now I spoke at least four presentably, and preferred English, because it was generally easier.

"You still have an accent, though," she said, turning her attention wholly to me. She gave me an easy smile, her head tilting slightly to take me in. "Kind of cute, if you ask me."

12

W hat in the holy hell was wrong with me?

You didn't tell a vampire he was...cute. Scary, most definitely. Forbidding...maybe, if I wanted to piss him off. But "cute" had to rank somewhere up there between calling him weak or a coward.

Which meant I did what any smart girl would do: I completely changed the subject.

"Where do we land?"

I hadn't asked before, because, honestly, the whole situation seemed surreal, and I didn't really think I'd actually be making this trip. Now that we were in the air, the prospect of an adventure seemed a bit more concrete.

"Edinburgh, of course."

Excitement tickled my stomach as I mentally ticked off at least four distilleries close by. I'd dreamed of Scotland since I was little, from the stories Great-Granddaddy told, to travel books Dad had lying around.

"What time does this meeting of yours start?" I was already mapping out our route, the shortest distance with the most distilleries. It wasn't even that hard, since there were so many.

"Not until midnight."

"Wow, good thing that's not clichéd, or anything." I watched Forge's eyes crinkle with laughter. "But good, we'll have time visit a distillery or two," I casually suggested. "Since I'm doing you a favor and all, you can indulge me, right?"

For a second, I thought he'd deny me, but Forge in the air was definitely more laid-back than Forge on the ground.

Of course, I should have known there'd be stipulations to him agreeing.

"Only if you manage to keep me from guessing every single thought that pops into your head." He looked at his watch. "Starting right now."

I focused my entire will on my facial muscles, praying my version of inscrutable was the same as Forge's. It must have passed muster, because after a glance, he leaned back —looking all king of the world—and got serious.

"First off," he said, "we have to arrive at eleven thirty, so it's just shy of clichéd. Secondly, I need to set down some ground rules for tonight."

"All right. Shoot."

"You do not leave my side. We will be seated together, but you do not leave your chair for any reason. You will read any vampire's thoughts that are easily accessible, but you will not speak until we are safely back in the plane. If anything happens to me, I have a...friend who will get you out."

It was taking a lot of effort to keep a straight face, and I must have misunderstood that last part. "Those are a lot of rules, Forge. You know how I feel about that."

That self-satisfied, smug look never left his face. "Your eyebrow is twitching, Selena."

I locked down my errant eyebrow. "Plus, that's too many rules for just one night. I thought this might be fun, but you're making it sound more like a job than an adventure."

I wasn't prepared for the way his face tightened up. I seemed to have a habit of pissing him of, especially when I wasn't even trying.

"This is not a lark, Selena. What I'm asking you to do..." His voice trailed off before he looked away. He raked his hand through his hair before he continued, "Tonight will be dangerous, even more so after you crossed paths with Dobson. The truth is, I shouldn't have involved you in my affairs, but I was...desperate."

I didn't like where this conversation was going. Forge sounded almost ominous. And the fact he'd allowed the word *desperate* to slip out meant that maybe this was.

"What are you not telling me? I mean, I know what I'm *supposed t*o do. But I never asked why."

"When there is a serious clan matter to decide, the twenty most powerful families gather in Edinburgh, Scotland. We call it Assembly—think of it as judge, jury and executioner, all around one table. They decide only the most serious cases."

"Why are we going to *this* particular meeting?" My feeling of vague disquiet began to grow, especially when Forge avoided my eyes completely.

"The Assembly only tries cases that deserve the death penalty."

"You are one of the judges?" *Please, please tell me he's one of the good guys...good vampires. Please don't let me have made a giant mistake.*

"I'm afraid not, Selena. I'm the one on trial."

"You didn't think to mention that right off the bat?" I was waffling between fear and anger, all while trying to keep my face expressionless, because, you know—*Scotland trip*. If only my dream vacation didn't involve a meeting with the deadly vampires who wanted to kill Forge.

"Actually," I said, finally settling on anger, "Scotland is quickly losing its cachet for me. Why didn't you tell me this from the very beginning?"

"Would you have agreed to it? Even to save your company?"

I thought about it. "Yes. I would have. Because even though it makes this adventure a little less...attractive, I owe you, and we Langstons—"

"Pay our debts. Yes, I've heard that somewhere before," Forge responded quietly, but the jab lacked the usual smugness. He drummed his fingers on the arm of his seat, involved in some internal debate before he shook his head. "You wouldn't have come, Selena. You would have heard the truth and walked away. I wouldn't have blamed you, not one bit. This meeting of the clan has been a long time coming. When I saw what you could do, I looked at you like my last chance."

"How am I supposed to help you, anyways? It's not like... Did you do what they think you did?" I asked quickly. God, I didn't even want to know. "I don't see how knowing everyone's thoughts will help you."

"I killed another vampire—it was a long time ago, and it wasn't a mistake; it was revenge. I had grounds for killing him. Unfortunately, he was the Elder's offspring."

"Okay, maybe we should have done a little more work in the terminology department. What's the difference between you and an Elder?" I nodded to Forge's watch. "How much time do we have?" I felt like I was heading to finals and didn't even know what classes I'd enrolled in.

"Five hours, and it's not complicated, Selena. All you need to do—"

"Explain things to me, or I won't step off this plane. I don't operate on this whole *shoot from the hip* approach. I prefer to have a solid plan before going in."

"How well do these solid plans of your usually work out?"

"Not well, but I'm not walking in there blind, either. Terminology lesson, Forge." Jeez, mind-reading vampires I'd signed up for, but this? The odds were beginning to look really, really bad.

"An Elder is a vampire who is older and more powerful than any other. At any one time, there is only one in existence, and, for our kind, his word is law."

"That doesn't sound like a good person to cross. I assume you had a really good reason for killing his offspring?"

"He killed Mara, my Maker. I killed him in return."

A shadow went over Forge's face when he mentioned Mara's name, and then I knew we were opening up a serious can of worms. While I got all caught up in who Mara had been to Forge—complete with a stab of jealousy—I managed, "Huh. That seems like a pretty good reason."

Vengeance usually ranked pretty high on the payback list. Humans took it seriously, and I'd just bet vampires took it to heart.

Or so I assumed.

13

_____

Reluctantly, I cherry-picked through the circumstances that brought us to Scotland. There was no way I'd tell Selena everything. Hiding one's worst inclinations from those who meant—were beginning to mean—something to them was practically the only human thing I'd carried over to this life.

Never mind Mara and I had been lovers.

Never mind the fact the Elder had almost killed me that night as well.

Never mind the fact the Elder was finally pursuing his vendetta.

I wasn't about to lay my entire life out in front of Selena. Not when parts of it were so ugly. Not when she wouldn't understand. The more I thought this through, the more I knew I should never have involved her in this. I'd been blinded by her ability. Blinded by her.

But that wasn't fair. I'd been too focused on using her to get me out of this jam, and not weighing the consequences. In truth, it had been so long since I'd worried about anyone other than myself, I'd forgotten how. But the thought of putting Selena in danger, the thought of any of my kind getting anywhere near her, brought out a primal, territorial response.

"I've managed to stave off the Elder for many years. Blackmail, you see, works better than gold among my kind. But I don't have my leverage anymore, and it appears the Elder has run out of patience."

"What happened to your leverage?" she asked.

"He's dead," I answered. "I didn't know it until they sent Dobson after me." Or rather, as soon as Dobson had materialized inside my *goddamned house*, I knew Jackson was dead. There was no other explanation for it. The Elder had killed him, and now was coming for me.

"Dobson...the washed-out vampire that looked like he wanted to have me for a snack?"

"Yes," I told her drily. "Him."

"You threatened to rip his head off, if I remember correctly," Selena pointed out, her tone every bit as droll as mine. "Stopped him in his tracks."

"He'd better have stopped. He was ten feet away from you." *Ten fucking feet...*

Jackson might be dead, and the hold I had over the Elder gone, but I still had contacts in Scotland. People I could rely on. If I didn't, I would never have brought Selena.

"That was too close."

"Yeah," she said soberly, her face tightening up just enough that I knew he'd really frightened her. "He was. I thought I was a goner. But then you showed up. Always saving me from something, or so it seems."

"Happy to oblige." I kept my words light, but just the way she'd said it made me hard. I shifted position before she noticed. Damn, all these years and I was as suave as a schoolboy.

She shook her head, her hair tumbling all around. "What am I doing here, Forge? I should be home, running the distillery, falling asleep before nine so I can get up early to check on the mash. This is way over my head. The only reason I'm here is..."

My chest constricted. Of course there was only one reason. "Because of the loan."

"No, actually, that's not it at all." Selena tilted her head, observing my face intently. "I guess you could say it was curiosity. I grew up hearing about you. You were a legend, like some kind of knight in shining armor who saved the company and cemented the Langston family's futures."

"I'm no knight, I can assure you of that." I didn't want to hear another word about Langston family gossip. "Selena, we've been over this, and I don't want to hear any more—"

She completely ignored me. "But to me, you were always more than a legend. Do you know how many times I've stared at your painting, speculating about who you really were?" She ducked her head. "I've wondered about you for years, Forge. Did you ever think," she added softly, "I just used the money as an excuse to meet you?"

As I struggled for some pithy comeback to the bomb-shell she'd just dropped, she smiled at me, breaking her expressionless visage. "Which means there's no way I'd pass up a chance to go to Scotland with you. Now that I can read minds—*and* keep a straight face while doing it—I want to find out what I can do. What you *taught* me to do."

Watching her face transform back to a serene, blank slate, I couldn't help but agree. "Maybe you *are* ready." Still, I wondered what we'd be walking into tonight. I was stronger than anyone else there, except the Elder. Given it had been years since our paths had crossed, I might even give him a go.

If I wasn't one hundred percent sure Selena would be safe at my side, I'd never have allowed this to progress so far. I was powerful, but I wasn't about to get cocky. After nearly two hundred years, the Elder had decided to come after me. I had to know why, or this would never end.

Which was where Selena came in—I needed her to read their minds and find out.

"I brought you something," I told her, surveying her perfectly mundane jeans and sweatshirt. "It's in the bedroom, and I hope it's the right size."

Her eyebrows twitched slightly, then settled back into place on her blank visage. "Gifts *and* a trip. You're too good to me, Forge."

"Just look in the bedroom," I told her, before I picked her up and carried her back there myself. Just the thought of her splayed out on my bed... I could almost imagine what she tasted like, a mix of musk and sweetness, and my mouth watered.

She blew me a kiss before she shut the door, then I heard a muffled squeal. Hopefully the dress fit her as well as the shoes. Vampires were a vicious lot, but they loved their fancy clothes, and if Selena was to fit in, she'd have to dress the part.

When Selena emerged in the green silk gown, which showed off every perfect curve, I knew my face showed exactly what I was thinking. "You look beautiful," I said, the words slipping out of my mouth while my brain was catching up. She was stunning. A woman made for expensive clothes and private jets.

A woman made for me, I told myself—before reminding myself that I was a dead man walking.

14

Forge and I practiced the mind-shielding thing for a couple of hours before I begged off with a headache. In truth, I was tired of having my brain poked like a pincushion. My mindset was that I was either ready, or I wasn't—and I'd be better off conserving my energy until tonight.

He'd changed as well, into a shirt that cost more than my car, and slacks that I wanted to run my fingers over. A leather jacket was thrown over the seat behind him.

Now we were sitting in opposite seats, two dollars on the table between us, and I was trying not to crack a smile as we tried to out-stare each other. The dress was hiked up so I could cross my legs, and I had my whisky balanced on my knee. Forge was doing his king-of-everything-I-survey pose, looking for all the world like an actual king.

The plane took that moment to hit turbulence, and I blinked.

"Hah," Forge said, surging forward triumphantly. "You lost."

He shot out his hand and collected my dollar as we hit

another pocket of turbulence. The plane dropped like a stone, my stomach along with it, my whisky hitting the floor just a second before I did. My fingers splayed out on the floor as the plane was caught in a freefall. I didn't look up until we leveled out.

"Selena," Forge said, his face inches from mine. "You're perfectly safe. It's just a bit of weather."

I couldn't stop shaking. I couldn't even think, I was so rattled. He carefully lifted me up, then set me back into the seat, shifting until he was beside me. He wasn't exactly warm, but he was comforting, and when his arms went around me, I shivered for an entirely different reason.

"I didn't know you were afraid of flying," he whispered into my hair. "I'm sorry."

"I always think I'll get better at it," I muttered miserably. "But then I get on a plane and I wish I hadn't. I really thought this would be different."

I went to pull away, but he wrapped his arms around me tighter. I finally gave up and sank against his chest. Nestled into him, I could almost forget we were in a tin can hurtling through the air. Soon enough, my stomach settled and my nerves evened out. Not that he'd save me from a crash, but damn, there was something about being held in Forge's arms that made me feel safe.

"We're only about an hour out. Which means we have important details to decide on. Like what you want to do first? Edinburgh is a big city, and unfortunately, we won't have a lot of time."

"Don't you... Shouldn't we get ready for tonight?" I asked him. "There's an awful lot riding on us being prepared." Suddenly I didn't feel at all prepared, not if I could be shaken up by a little turbulence. I looked at him, chewing my lip before I reminded myself to stop.

"We are ready, and tonight is a long way away. Which distillery do you want to visit first?"

My heart raced. "We won't have time to go to Hadrian's in Stirling, obviously. But could we possibly squeeze in Cameron?" Hadrian's operation extended into the States and gave us a run for our money, but Cameron whisky was a small, private distillery, only producing a few thousand bottles a year. It was my very favorite, and I wanted to get a glimpse of their stills.

Forge actually cracked a cocky smile and strode to the door to the cockpit. Like he was telling a cab driver to drop him at the curb, he told the pilot, "Change of plans. File a new flight plan for Stirling, then another one for Perth.

"Now you don't have to choose," he told me, once again gathering me against him, as if we'd done this a hundred times. With his other hand, he sent a series of texts, then tucked his phone back in his pocket. I wasn't sure what I'd expected, but landing in Stirling wrapped up in Forge's arms was not it.

Nor was I prepared when he handed me a long, warm coat, something I'd not thought to bring.

I threw it on and followed him down to the bottom of the stairs, where he turned and offered me his hand to guide me the last few steps. A car was waiting, and I ducked under his arm as he held the door open, sliding in beside me.

"Welcome back, Mr. Forge," the driver said, giving us both an enthusiastic nod in the rearview. "Good of you to visit us again in Stirling." I had to use considerable brain-power to unravel the words from the accent, but Forge was way ahead of me.

"Good to be here, Bobby. I hope Seamus knows how much I appreciate this, especially on short notice." Forge settled himself so his thigh lay the full length of mine. I didn't move away.

"He's waiting for you in the main cask house. I believe he's tapping a special barrel, just for you."

"Ach, I appreciate it, Bobby," Forge murmured, then squeezed my knee.

It didn't take long before Forge's accent grew almost as thick as the driver's. He was practically speaking Gaelic by the time we pulled up in front of an imposing stone building with *Hadrian's Distillery* emblazoned on the front, the cobbled street in front of it just adding to the charm.

I'd spent the entire ride glued to the window, watching little towns and craggy mountains fly by as we maneuvered through the narrow roads. Forge and Bobby never stopped going back and forth, sounding more like old friends than driver and fare.

Forge got out first, thoroughly scrutinizing the building, then the street, before offering me his hand. Sliding mine into his, it felt natural, as if we'd been doing this forever. Not for the first time I wondered why, exactly, I was more comfortable with a vampire than someone of my own species.

"Bastian." The owner—I assumed it was the owner—pulled Forge into a bear hug, and while they spoke quietly, I looked around the inside of the building. It was beautiful, with a layer of history that I could never hope to duplicate in Philadelphia, but the best thing was that I smelled mash.

"Are you brewing right now?" I asked.

The owner turned to me as if noticing me for the first time, and his look of shock was priceless.

"Seamus, may I present Selena Langston, owner of Langston-Forge in Philadelphia."

Seamus winked at me, then took my hand and kissed it. "A good whisky, Langston-Forge, when we can get it."

"As is yours—one of my favorites, to be honest," I said.

"You hardly look old enough to drink, much less run a distillery." Seamus's voice dropped. "But when I heard your father passed, I was glad to see the company stayed in the family. There were rumors it would be broken up and sold."

"I couldn't let that happen."

"I would think not." Seamus snorted. "When whisky is in your blood, you can't get it out. Money isn't everything, you know, but a board... All they know is money. They don't know shit about the business."

"True," I told him, "But to be fair, none of them grew up in the business—to them, we're just another company." I was aware of Forge's hand slipping from mine as he went to the small table and sniffed the unlabeled bottle, then poured three glasses.

"A whisky brat, then, just like me."

I laughed. "I've heard of army brats, but never a whisky brat. But yes, I grew up at my dad's side at the distillery, learning as much as I could." Seamus reminded me of Granddad, with his irreverent attitude and shooting me a mischievous wink after every comment.

Seamus chuckled and rubbed his hands together. "Let's see how much you've learned, then. Tell me what you think, once you taste my finest creation." Our table consisted of an old barrel and three mismatched chairs, but the complex cachet of the whisky reached my nose as Forge pressed a glass into my hand.

Seamus sat down heavily. "Let's see how much you know, Selena Langston."

I hid my smile. What Seamus didn't know was that I'd studied his operation thoroughly. I was always looking at my competition, and Hadrian's was my biggest, in terms of quantity. Hadrian's was well run, and they distributed to every corner of the earth, while still maintaining their quality. After meeting Seamus, I could see why.

I took a tentative sip, letting the whisky warm my mouth and burn my nose before I swallowed.

"Smoky, but without the bitter bite, so you used peat to dry the barley. I can taste the oak... European oak barrels, I believe. And the citrus..." I took another sip and truly savored the loveliness of it this time. "Double-charred barrels."

Seamus clapped his hands. "That is very good, Miss Langston. But all I had to see was the look on your face to know you truly enjoy it." He poured another round, and we all raised our glasses. "*Sláinte mhath.*" The clink of our glasses sounded like a bell.

"What do you like most about making whisky?" Forge asked, his dark eyes searching mine over our glasses.

"I guess for me, it's when I go somewhere and see a bottle of Langston-Forge, and I know either my dad or my grandpop bottled that. Knowing that really brings our family history home. I like knowing I can make a whisky that people truly love, and somehow, it makes the world seem like a smaller place."

Something sparked in Forge's eyes, just before he hid it away. "A very good reason to enjoy what you do."

Seamus and Forge began a good-natured banter back and forth while I enjoyed the simple pleasure of whisky and good company. It had been a long time since I'd stopped and allowed myself to relax. Years, maybe, if I was honest, and it felt wonderful to let the warmth sink into me, to let Forge put his arm around my shoulder.

Bobby drove us back to the airport, and when we

landed in Perth, my cheeks were still heated from the whisky and I was feeling quite content. I let Forge bundle me into the waiting car, and then fell into a blissful sort of fog as he and our new driver fell into a string of unintelligible Gaelic.

"Selena, we're here."

I lifted my head off his shoulder—somehow, I'd fallen asleep on him—and looked around. Cameron Distillery was nestled in a deep gorge between two sheer spires of granite. Smoke billowed out of the tall chimney stack, and I felt Forge's fingers intertwine with mine as he tugged me out of the car into the cool, pine-scented air.

Of every other whisky I'd ever tasted, Cameron was my hands-down favorite. This distillery was even older than mine, and their blend was the whisky I hoped to rival with Dad's special batch—and all the ones that came after. *I can't believe I'm actually here.* I spun in a circle, my arms thrown wide, the coat flying out like a cape.

"This place is...magical."

For a second, Forge froze, then cupped his hand beneath my elbow. "It is, isn't it," he murmured as we made our way to the building. Surprisingly, Forge didn't knock, just pushed through the door, bringing me inside with him.

Cameron was everything I'd imagined a Scottish operation to be. Stone floors, high plastered ceilings and a thick, palpable layer of history over the entire place. Forge flicked on the lights, bathing the room in the golden light of old incandescent bulbs. "I'll fetch glasses and a bottle," he said as he strode away, leaving me to wander.

This distillery didn't strive to be on any Scottish Highlands tour—it was a bare-bones operation with no intention to impress. Somehow, not what I'd expected. I did remember when I'd researched Cameron that their online presence had been meager, just a landing page with a generic picture of the Highlands.

I paused in front of a faded, stained photograph. It was clearly the distillery's staff, gathered out in front of this building, arms thrown over each other's shoulders. The date scratched in the corner was 1921.

Right in the center of the group was Forge, looking exactly the same as he did right now, except without his usual, forbidding scowl. Somehow, he looked—if not as happy as everyone around him—content. A half-smile curved his lips up, and his eyes looked lighter, brighter.

God, he's handsome, I thought, my heart leaping at the quiet joy in his face.

"That was a good crew," he commented softly over my shoulder, and I jumped a mile into the air. He slid a glass into my hand, brushing his fingers against mine as he did.

"Jeez, Forge, don't sneak up on me like that." I hoped he wasn't doing that creepy sliding thing that Dobson did, but I sure hadn't heard any footsteps. "Or should I say...the reclusive owner of the Cameron Distillery?"

"That's me, guilty as charged."

I mock-punched him in the shoulder, almost spilling whisky everywhere. "You could have told me," I said, trying to figure out why he'd hide this from me. "Although it explains a lot. Like why you loaned Ambrose the money in the first place."

"We were competitors here in Scotland, small-time, unlicensed distillers, but we were happy enough. As taxes and English oversight increased, it became problematic to produce enough to keep ourselves afloat. We decided to go to America and try our luck there. I had no intention of staying; I only went to see Ambrose get established. But...then things changed."

"You mean *you* changed?" He did look almost...happy in the photograph, and I wondered why he had stayed in the States. Especially when this place was so wonderful.

"That, amongst other things. I liked America. I appreciated the freedom it offered, and watching a new country grow was...*exciting*. I stayed, until one night when I..." As his voice trailed off, I remembered his Maker's name.

"Then you met Mara," I prompted, willing my voice not to harden.

"You remembered her name." He sounded genuinely surprised. *Well, yes, since she's my competition.* Or who I'd begun to think of as my competition. Or whatever she was. Forge nodded, his black hair spilling over his forehead. "Yes, I met Mara Sheldon, and she changed me."

"How does that even work?"

"We became lovers—unheard of at the time, a vampire and a human, but Mara was never one for conventions. Eventually, I decided immortality would give me time to accomplish everything I wanted to do. She changed me into a vampire. It's a painful process, but Mara helped me through it. We remained together for years." He paused. "Although I'm sure you've figured that out."

I was too busy struggling with my jealousy to even respond.

"We were together when she crossed paths with Xavier, the Elder's offspring. He tried to... Well, long story short, they fought, and Xavier killed her. Mara wasn't a fighter. She didn't stand a chance."

Forge was staring through the room, absently swirling the whisky in his glass. "I hunted him down and killed him. Murdering an Elder's offspring was an unforgivable offense, but I had evidence the Elder couldn't afford to have exposed.

He and I came to an agreement: I would stay in America and never set foot in Scotland again."

"And yet here we are," I said drily, sure now that this whole thing was a giant mistake. Maybe he was still in love with Mara. He sure sounded in love with her. What I wouldn't give to hear that tender tone in his voice when he spoke of me.

"Only because he decided to kill Jackson, my only living witness, and call in my debt by dredging up the old crime and using it summon me before the Assembly." He was watching me intently, clearly trying to make up his mind about something. "You're my ace in the hole." As if he'd come to a decision, Forge threw back his drink in one go. "Or, at least, you *were*."

"I'm right here, Forge, and I've been practicing for weeks to get this right. Not only can I handle this, I have every intention of attending that meeting tonight."

"That will be impossible, since I've decided you'll be flying back to Philadelphia."

"Oh no you don't. We had a deal..."

"Your loan is forgiven." His voice hardened. "Don't worry —you don't owe me a penny, Selena." He nodded to someone over my shoulder, and I heard the door close quietly behind me. "The driver will take you take you back to the plane, and you'll fly home tonight."

I was trying to come up with something—anything—to convince him to let me go to that meeting. Damn it, this wasn't about the money. This was about my abilities and what I could do with them.

"But before you go...I need you to wear this, Selena. Never take it off, and don't show it to anyone." In his palm was a beautiful gold pendant of a serpent swallowing his tail.

"Turn around and let me put this on you." I did, not understanding why he'd changed his mind so abruptly, and trying to buy some time to firm up my argument for staying. Somehow, I had the feeling that I wouldn't be able to sway him.

Forge hooked the clasp behind my neck, his fingers skimming my nape before I let my hair back down. Instead of stepping away, he settled his hands on my bare shoulders, one of his thumbs absently drawing circles on my collarbone. God, his hands felt so good on me, and for an instant, my mind wandered back to the bedroom on the plane, complete with a king-sized bed.

I picked up the pendant for a closer look. "It's an ouroboros, isn't it?"

Forge nodded, a strange expression on his face as he took in the necklace, then my face. "It looks as if it were made for you."

"Was it, Forge?" I asked, searching for why he was giving me the brush-off, and what could have possibly changed these past few hours. "Was this made for me?"

He ducked his head, whether in embarrassment or dismay, I didn't know. When his gaze met mine again, his face was indecipherable, but my breath picked up when he finally admitted, "Yes, it was. I had it commissioned."

"When?"

"The day you came to see me."

"But that would mean..." I broke off, completely at a loss. "Explain."

"I'm part of a...call it a loose society of like-minded vampires. Not all of us are savages like Dobson. Some of us have a vested interest in helping humanity." He drew an audible breath. "Humans like you."

I felt the floor fall out from beneath my feet. "What do you mean *like me*? Like people who own distilleries, or *people who can read vampire minds*?" What was he implying? That this wasn't just a business deal?

"Yes, Selena, special humans who have abilities, mental, physical...any humans we deem special enough to offer our patronage and protection."

"Protection?" I scoffed. "I don't need protection, Forge." My temper began to heat up as I added, "Especially from you. I'm perfectly capable of handling anything that comes my way."

"You were," he easily agreed. "Until you showed up at my house with a bottle of whisky and a proposal. Now you're in my world, and you need me, Selena, like it or not."

He lifted his eyes to the ceiling, then looked back at me, his gaze hard. "The truth is, you aren't ready for this meeting. Maybe with more practice...or more time. But I can't allow you to walk in there to be eaten alive by those monsters."

"Can't or won't?" I asked. I should have seen this coming. Mercurial changes in plans were what Forge was best at. "Someone should have told you that the worst possible beginning to any relationship is with a bunch of secrets. Shit, practically everything you've told me was a lie."

"Not a lie, just not entirely the truth."

"Which in my world is also known as a lie."

For a minute, we were at a stalemate, until the driver cleared his throat behind us. He said something in Gaelic, Forge said something back, rather snippily, I thought, and then we went back to staring at one another.

Did Forge think I was only doing this for the money? Of course, this had all started with the loan, but now...now I wanted to help him beat the Assembly and that creeper Dobson.

I wanted to be part of a team, like Batman and Robin,

me being a smarter and more kick-ass partner than Robin ever could be. Besides, it turned out—now that I actually knew about him—Forge and I were a lot alike.

Shitty circumstances, general lack of trust in our fellow species and...well, having a death sentence hanging over your head was definitely worse than crushing debt, but everything else was the same.

So why was he kicking me to the curb right before the big event? A shiver of doubt ran through me. Maybe he really *didn't* think I could do it. Maybe he thought I wasn't good enough.

Not good enough. I snorted to myself. *I'm always good enough.* I had to be, especially when I followed after Brandon, who was a perfect fuck-up. To counteract my brother's badness, I became the best, as if that might somehow fix Brandon.

At least it made Dad happy.

My brother spent his teenage years stealing, lying, wrecking cars, and that was just the tip of the iceberg. Then he graduated to bank robbery and heroin, finally finding a home in compulsive gambling. It wasn't long before his drug and gambling habits spiraled out of control. Cue the loan shark, and cue putting the company up as collateral.

Cue Selena trying to fix it all.

I was left juggling the company and trying to figure out how Dad got involved in Brandon's mess in the first place. Then came the debts, and the hostile board, and that was when I went to Forge, figuring at this point, what did I have to lose? A lot, as it turned out.

"Don't you have anything to say?" I didn't know what I hoped for, maybe for him to beg me to stay, to which I'd spin on my heel and leave him hanging like the righteous bitch I was.

"When I met you—when I realized you could read my thoughts—all I thought about was how I could use you to outmaneuver my old clan. But you have no place in our world, and now, you're going home."

Not the answer I'd hoped for, and that probably would have been the end of it.

I might have gone home, forgotten about Forge and gone back to running my company.

Until there was a wet, rasping sound behind us. I turned just in time to see the driver—bleeding from the neck—drop to the floor in a heap.

A stream of blood ran down Dobson's chin as he grinned at us.

Dobson's pale eyes flickered over me as I raised my shield and immediately felt Forge close the space between us. Then he pressed me to him, an arm across my belly.

"If you touch her, you're dead," Forge warned Dobson in a low growl, his arm tightening around me.

"Of course," Dobson said easily, blood dripping from his chin onto the front of his shirt as his weird eyes remained fixed on me. *He really is an asshole,* I thought, as my gaze strayed to the dying driver twitching on the floor. "I'll get my chance...sooner or later."

"Damn it, Forge..." I murmured, sinking further into Forge's embrace. Right now, he was my only chance of survival, and I damn well knew it.

"Later. Take my hand and don't let go." He wrapped a hand around my forearm, and I shifted closer to him, no intention whatsoever of letting him out of my sight.

"Transportation will be here in a moment. The Elder prefers to do things the old way." Dobson's fangs dripped. "I will meet you there."

What in the hell does that even mean? I thought, Forge's hand sliding down to clasp mine.

"He only means we will be taking a car, Selena," Forge murmured. "Remember our lessons, and don't—*for even a moment*—forget the sort of monsters that surround you."

I wouldn't. Not after seeing the hunger in Dobson's eyes, nor the sense of malevolence he'd brought in with him. There would be no arguing with this one, no begging, nothing that would forestall the death lurking in Dobson's eyes. He enjoyed killing, and only Forge stood between me and those teeth. I schooled my face into an impenetrable mask and reinforced my defenses as Dobson poked around. A cool, comforting sensation swept through me as Forge added his shield over mine.

"Shall we?" Forge asked Dobson, while I heard the heavy crunch of tires on the gravel outside. Was I heading to my execution? Or was this just a ride to the meeting?

Desperately, I formed the questions in my head, hoping Forge heard them.

Where are we going? To the meeting? Even internally, my voice sounded shrill.

Yes. Calm down. Your face is giving you away.

Fine, I mentally snapped. *How am I supposed to do everything at once? There's fucking blood dripping down the front of him.*

You've been practicing for this, Selena. Forge's voice became a dark, soothing presence in my head. *Stay by my side and keep your mind protected at all times. If you hear anything you deem important...tell me immediately.*

Fine, but I'm not doing any weird stuff. Well, weirder than this already is, I amended.

Dobson kept his eyes on us until we were shut in the car, and when I looked back, he was gone. Although we couldn't see the driver—the privacy window was up—he took his time piloting the huge sedan through the roads, as if we weren't on a deadline. *At least I saw Scotland before I died. Check one thing off the old bucket list.* As soon as we reached the outskirts of Edinburgh, Forge squeezed my hand, hard enough to get my attention.

He leaned in, close enough that I felt his breath on my cheek, and I turned my head, brushing my lips against his. Accident or on purpose, I didn't know, but I licked my bottom lip, tasting the trace Forge had left behind.

His eyes flared open in surprise, but then they grew hesitant, and I wondered how much worse things were about to get.

I never wanted you to have to see this, but now there's no avoiding it.

He didn't let go of my hand as he began changing. I realized that whatever I thought I knew about him and his kind, my popcorn version of a vampire had nothing to do with the real Forge.

He went from broody and unapproachable to frightening, his eyes growing black, his fangs—something I'd barely glimpsed before—on full display. They had to be an inch long. The planes on his face grew sharper, more defined, until Forge hardly looked human at all. There were dark splotches beneath his skin, but it was those eyes that kept pulling me back. Seeing him transform excited me, and God help me, I loved every minute of it.

———

INSTEAD OF WORRYING about the impending meeting, I was fighting a war inside myself over whether to be thankful Selena was with me, or pissed over the fact I hadn't gotten her to safety in time. If I'd been a few minutes quicker, she'd be headed back to the plane, and I could deal with the Elder bullshit on my own.

The second Dobson appeared, my heart had almost stopped beating as I realized he was heading straight for her.

Toward everything I had to lose.

When Dobson had the nerve to look her up and down like a piece of meat, I swore I'd pop those eyeballs right out of his head with my thumbs.

"If you touch her, you're dead." The threat slipped out of my mouth as I prepared myself to take this fucker out, but unfortunately, Dobson obligingly obeyed. Still, I didn't feel comfortable until Selena was pressed against me, her heart beating a mile a minute.

Selena tried to argue, but before she said anything damning, I quietly warned her, "Later. Take my hand and don't let go." Just to be sure she obeyed, I gripped her arm, grateful she moved closer instead of fighting me.

Dobson closely followed the move, his eyes lighting up as he found some leverage he could use against me. He made a comment strictly to rattle Selena, then dropped the Elder's name, as if he actually knew the asshole personally. When he added the bit about the Elder, Dobson bared his teeth, as if he'd win this pissing contest.

I clasped her hand firmly, trying to put her mind at ease before I reminded her, "Remember our lessons, and don't —*for even a moment*—forget the sort of monsters that surround you."

As we made our way to the car, I surveyed her face. Set in determination, but other than that, no one but me would be able to discern her innermost thoughts.

While I'd intended to send her away to protect her, there

wasn't any way to safely extricate her from this situation. I could easily kill Dobson and the driver, but it was a given that one of them would go for her, and she could get hurt. Which meant I'd keep her close, where I could protect her. Even with my misgivings, I couldn't deny that she felt like a natural at my side.

Panic rippled through her body and through her thoughts, panic I tried to soothe away.

Where are we going? To the meeting? Selena's voice was filled with fear, but she kept her eyes pointed forward. Her mask slipped for a moment, revealing trembling lips.

Yes. Calm down. Your face is giving you away.

Fine. Her voice turned sharp as nails as she clamped her lips together in a straight, unwavering line. *But I'm not doing any weird stuff. Well, weirder than this already is.*

I fought the urge to chuckle, and we both watched out the windows as the city's outermost buildings appeared. I had to change—I had no choice. We were walking into the lion's den, and I intended to go in at full strength. *The Elder wants a fight? I'll be happy to give him one.*

It didn't escape me that, once again, I was going up against the Elder over a woman, but then again, I couldn't think of a better reason. To get her attention, I gave Selena's hand a squeeze. When her eyes flew to mine, I saw the glimmer of fear in them before she extinguished it.

I meant to whisper in her ear, to tell her everything would be okay. I meant to lie and pretend tonight was under control. But as I leaned in, she turned her head, her lips a velvet brush against mine. Blood rushed through me in a hot spike of lust as her tongue flicked out and licked her bottom lip, her eyes going dark.

For a moment I struggled with just how easy it would be to kill the driver and take her back to the plane. To be between her legs, lapping her up, to drink from her throat as she writhed beneath me. Then I realized I could have her. We could have each other, once the Elder and Dobson were out of the way. But only if she knew what I really was.

I didn't want you to have to see this, but now there's no avoiding it.

I held her hand as I loosened my control and began transforming. Instantly the stale air in the car was filled with a subtle, spicy perfume. Selena's scent. I'd expected her to shrink back, to show a trace of fear, distaste at minimum, as she watched my face change from human to something other.

What she didn't see was the increased speed, the enhanced senses, and—because Selena was so close to me, her sweet scent filling my senses—a pounding need to sink my teeth, and my cock, into her right here and now. We vampires were nothing but savage beasts, despite our thin veil of civility.

I opened my mouth to apologize, to make some comment to cover up my reaction, but her perfume turned sweeter, spicier, desire tinged with sexual interest, and fuck me if that wasn't the sweetest thing I'd ever smelled.

But if I smelled it, so would the others, which would bring nothing but trouble. All we needed was her drug-like scent whipping the entire Assembly into bloodlust.

It would be easy enough to kill the driver, drive to the plane and put her on it, even if it was kicking and screaming over my shoulder. But now, Dobson knew who she was. He'd hunt her down, whether it was in two weeks or twenty years, and I couldn't take that chance.

No, I'd let this play out. I was confident I could handle the Assembly, and as for Dobson...I was itching for some payback. The Elder would be trickier, and as curious as I was to find out why he'd reneged on our two-century-old deal, I was determined he'd never get close to Selena.

I ran a hand up her arm and rested it on her shoulder, feeling the fragility of the bones. Her green eyes flew to mine, a look of surprise curving her lips into a half-smile.

When we arrive, think of it like the curtains going up. You need to become a completely different person.

Watch me, Forge, she quipped, without her face showing a glimmer of humor. *Just you watch me.*

16

CORRENNIE GARDENS, EDINBURGH

The car glided to a stop in front of a tall hedge enclosed by a stone wall. Just over the manicured top of the bushes, a stately, dark brick house jutted into a black sky. From what I'd seen driving in, this could be any street in the city. But this place had an aura of palpable evil, even though we were still in the car.

Forge gave my hand the barest squeeze, then ducked out as soon as the driver opened the door. After scanning the street, he motioned me forward and helped me out. The driver growled audibly as we passed, and Forge snarled back before he pulled me even closer.

As I drank in his cologne, I'd be lying if I said I regretted coming.

Adrenaline was racing through my veins like it never had before. With Forge so close, looking every inch a dangerous predator, I was teetering between edgy excitement and lust, probably totally inappropriate, but I couldn't help myself. Seeing Forge like this, in his element, was turning my insides to mush. But I appeared as sedate as

Forge while we slowly meandered our way to the front door, as if we were arriving for tea.

Or whatever they drank in Scotland. Hopefully something strong.

I was determined to do this, to get Forge the leverage he needed to escape the death penalty and get this Elder off his back. However, now that we were here, it occurred to me that I didn't actually know how to read vampire minds. Forge's voice just kind of appeared in my head.

Maybe, I thought, *we should have practiced the mind-reading part a bit more.*

I squashed my urge to thank the man who took my coat, as Forge mentally warned me, *You do not speak to anyone. Act as if they are beneath you.*

I did as he commanded, even though I was a little itchy following his orders without so much as one smart-ass comment. Obviously, he'd been right—obedience was really not my thing. Not that I'd ever tell him that. Why ruin what we had going?

In true vamp-cliché fashion, the other participants—a mix of men and slinky-looking women—were dressed in red and black, and I was grateful for this fancy dress and heels. At least I hadn't slunk in here in my sweatshirt and jeans. I also understood why Forge had been so insistent on me practicing.

Not so much as a twitch showed on anyone's face; they were a study in unreadable, brutal calm—the kind I could never hope to attain. Power thrummed in this room, also something I could never hope to compete with. The further in we went, the less confident I was that my training—all two weeks of it—would get me through tonight.

Maybe Forge had a point. Maybe I couldn't do this.

You can, Selena. You have something no one else in this room has, something they'd kill for. Forge's voice caressed my mind, so confident that I almost believed him.

I didn't let go of Forge's hand as he strode through the crowd, most parting to allow him passage, some averting their gaze, others looking me over with rapt interest, until I felt stripped naked.

Along the way I caught snippets of thoughts—mostly petty grievances—as we skirted the table. I stole a sideways glance to put faces with the voices. *So inconvenient, such short notice... Forge is finally going to get his... Who is that delicious-smelling human...*

I forced myself to remain impassive, to remember why we were here, and what rode on this meeting. We took two seats next to each other, and I made sure *my* leg fell against Forge's, savoring the now-familiar feeling of touching him. In response, he laid his hand on my thigh, making me instantly feel better.

Dobson, the asshole, slid in through a side door like the snake he was, took one look at me and licked his lips. I didn't need to read his mind to tell what he was thinking, especially when Forge's rage spiked in hot waves through my head. I did what any savvy woman did—I stared right at the smarmy blonde and pretended I didn't see him. His mocking smile dimmed a bit, and a rush of triumph went through me.

Somehow, this strange assembly reminded me of the Langston-Forge board—pompous, self-interested people who thought they ran the world. Of course, these vampires had teeth and could tear me apart, but the concept was the same. The realization brought clarity and took some of the edge off. Hell, I dealt with assholes like this every day.

Just like in the human world, the Elder showed up last, two huge, pit bull bodyguards taking up positions behind him. Classic power move that only worked on the newbs. I took note of the vampires who instantly took their seats, one of them sliding his cell phone into his pocket. The older—and I assumed more powerful—vampires took their good old time milling around, then choosing their seats strategically.

Dobson set his back against the wall behind the Elder, smirking. We were directly across from them, where I could keep my eye on them both. The internal hum of voices hadn't stopped since we'd arrived, and it was becoming harder and harder to sort through them, while keeping my gaze on Dobson and the Elder.

The Elder had some kind of bald and evil vibe going on, with a full-on turtleneck, the kind I hadn't seen since I was little, paired with a wool jacket with actual elbow patches. Someone seriously needed to bring this guy's wardrobe into the twentieth century.

Shit, at least Forge knew how to dress.

Thank you, Selena. Your approval means the world to me.

I squashed my smile and waited for the Elder's thoughts to float to me on the air, like the other's had, but I got nothing. He rapped his knuckles on the table, and instantly, the voices in my head—and those around the table—stopped.

He spoke in a gravelly voice, in a language I couldn't understand—at least, not until Forge began translating in my head.

He's welcoming the Assembly and going over the rules. For some reason, Forge skipped those, so I'd have to figure them out for myself, apparently. *Now he's asking for votes to move his motion forward.*

Around us, most of the participants raised a hand, or nodded. Two young ones' hands shot into the air. Jeez, teacher's pet, much?

Forge paused as they took a count, then continued his commentary. *He's listing out the charges: murder, torture and treason. Seems like he's hitting all the highlights. He must really want to bury me today.* I really didn't like the sound of that.

The Elder spoke again, his indifferent gaze skimming the table. The second his eyes fell on me, I felt it, the jolt traveling through me like I'd been plugged into an electric outlet. A corner of his mouth quirked up in pleasure before he struck. The crawling sensation encompassed my entire body, until all I heard was the scratchy wiggling of worms as they ate at my brain. He was scraping away my shield, a little bit at a time, and there was nothing I could do to stop him.

Put your head down. Break the eye contact.

Forge's deep, steady voice cut through the sensation, pulled me back to the here and now, and I did as he said, the vampire still trying to dig his way inside. Forge's shield locked into place over mine, creating an impenetrable barrier that made me feel safe. I hadn't thought I'd need his help, not until I experienced the power of the Elder.

Hang on, Selena. He can't touch you now.

I knew Forge wouldn't let him get to me. I knew he'd do everything he could to keep me safe. But I was afraid to tip our hand as the Elder poked and prodded at me, a cat with a canary. The Elder was scowling now, his careful mask gone, and he murmured something indecipherable to Forge.

Who didn't bother to translate, so it must have been bad.

The Elder finally gave up, shooting me a look that clearly said this wasn't over, then went back to droning on about Forge and—I assumed—all the really bad things he was going to do.

Forge's shield slid away, allowing snippets of the other vampires' voices in, and this time, I focused on Dobson. Not that I wanted to know what he was thinking; it just seemed like he was a major player in this charade.

Even though I knew what he sounded like, it took a bit of trial and error to pick him out of the vengeful crowd, most of whom hated Forge with a passion and were eager to see him get what was coming to him.

As I was here to ensure Forge did *not* get what may or may not be coming to him, I took it upon myself to figure out who wanted him dead and why. Unfortunately, the Elder would be the ideal target, but as I didn't speak his language, I was forced to focus on Dobson.

His running commentary about the meeting was interspersed with occasional images of Forge hanging upside down, blood dripping from everywhere. As disturbing as this was for me, killing Forge was obviously a favorite fantasy of Dobson's, because he imagined it more often than I was sure was normal. My takeaway was that he had unresolved Forge issues, and thus was a willing participant to all of this madness, so long as it ended with Forge dead.

But he wasn't a major player.

Dobson didn't realize he was also constantly thinking about the three vampires positioned just outside the room, ready to swoop down and throw us into the waiting truck. According to his somewhat gloating thoughts, the plan was to kill us both and leave Forge for the sun. Maybe there was some kind of poetic justice in conning him while he was conning us, but it remained to be seen which of us would have an opportunity to gloat. Even worse, I had to warn Forge of the impending attack, but was afraid of being overheard.

The Elder abruptly stopped talking, staring at Forge. Forge held his stare unflinchingly, and the Elder's face twisted in hatred. This time when he spoke, flecks of spittle coated the table between us, and I didn't have to speak his language to know he'd just pronounced judgment.

When that murderous gaze slid over to me, I made my move, praying no one else heard me.

Three men outside the room. Waiting to take us so Dobson can kill us.

Whether those two sentences were enough, I didn't know, but then Forge leaned back in his chair and stretched his arm across the back of mine, encircling my shoulders.

"Tell me, Meyer, why did it take you so long to kill Jackson? We made a deal, as I recall."

I almost snickered. "Meyer the Elder" sounded like a game show host's name.

This time, no translation was needed. "Jackson died in an unfortunate accident. As to *a deal*, I'm sure I don't know what you're talking about." It turned out the Elder's English was impeccable. "The entire clan agrees. Your offense—while long ago—demands recompense. All in favor?"

Every hand around us shot into the air.

Bunch of fucking kiss-asses.

"Separate him from his human and take him out back." He turned his calculating gaze on me. "Let us see what makes her unique enough that he brought her tonight."

Dobson's victorious look was enough that I knew we were in trouble, and he leaned down and whispered something in the Elder's ear that was clearly amusing. Then the meeting exploded as three vampires materialized in the room. One on either side of Forge, plus one directly behind me.

Blood and mayhem wasn't how I'd planned for tonight to go, but neither had I expected Forge's violent reaction when the vampires tried to separate us. My arm practically disappeared in the grip of a huge hand as I was yanked out of my seat and away from Forge. He tore the sleeve off my lovely dress, and in the melee, my necklace came loose, the pendant swinging wildly.

I was tossed around as I fought against his hold, until I finally landed on the floor, while the rest of the group shot to their feet, every eye fixed on my golden ouroboros pendant on full display.

The Elder's gaze went to it like a laser, a slow, cruel smile creasing his lined face.

Then the world went mad. I'd grown up around rough men, but nothing prepared me for three vampires fighting. In the blink of an eye, Forge destroyed the one who held my arm, then bared his fangs and launched himself at the other. Blood sprayed the side of my face as he drove my attacker into the wall behind us and ripped out his throat.

It was over in seconds, the attackers dead on the floor, Forge looking like it had never happened. Maybe that was why he'd worn black. He helped me off the floor, then reached over and gently tucked the necklace beneath my neckline. A red mark on the wall was all that was left of my attacker by the time Forge casually took his seat beside me once more.

I curled my hands into fists to stop my trembling, fighting to regain my calm demeanor. However, after Forge's demonstration, I was less worried about Dobson's plot to assassinate us. Dobson had gone an extra shade of pale, his skin matching his white hair as he sidled toward the exit like a rat.

"Touch her again and I'll kill you," Forge said, completely unruffled. I managed to contain my shocked reaction to a raised eyebrow. *Go me.* "Now...why did it take you two hundred years to grow balls big enough to come after me?" Forge smirked.

"Killing a vampire—no matter the circumstances—is punishable by death." Now the Elder sounded downright growly, which didn't seem to faze Forge one bit. The Elder gestured around the table at the rapt audience. "It's been voted on and agreed to. You will die for what you did."

But the whole time the Elder spoke, he wasn't looking at Forge at all. A sick feeling grew in my stomach as I realized his beady gaze was focused on me. "As for your Chosen..."

"She is not part of this, and is under the society's protection." His lip curled up, revealing dangerous-looking fangs. "*And mine.*" I froze as the Elder raked me with another covetous look.

That half-smile curled his lip again. "Despite what you think, convicted killers have no rights, including offering *protection* to humans. I find it interesting you took a Chosen under your wing. You never struck me as a humanitarian, Forge." The Assembly drew in a collective breath and leaned closer.

Shit, I think that's me...Chosen. Sounds like some kind of actual title.

Yet another thing I'd take up with Forge as soon as we got out of this. The bigger issue was I hadn't yet discovered anything that might help us. Maybe I should have stuck with making whisky, since I kind of sucked at this spy stuff.

Still, the night was young.

"I believe I was summoned," Forge said, straightening his blood-flecked cuffs, which I noticed had gold links that matched the necklace around my neck. "I was curious, I suppose, to see what my kind had devolved into these past centuries. I must say, you're an even worse lot than I expected."

There was death in Forge's face as he calmly pointed out, "As you can see, I can reduce your numbers considerably, should any of you lot piss me off." He leveled his cold stare at the Elder. "Including you.

"However," Forge went on, as if he hadn't just threatened everyone with death. Bloody death, from the look of his three victims. "I came here in good faith to get an explanation. Now, I expect an apology for attacking me on neutral ground. Once I have it, I'll return to America, never to set foot on Scottish soil again."

Only I caught the note of regret in that statement, a sure sign that I was finally starting to figure him out. It pissed me off that this pompous group of assholes had set their sights on Forge, going to all this trouble just to settle some old score. I shifted slightly in my chair, a move the Elder—and Dobson—tracked closely.

"Apology?" The Elder's voice was shaking. "I owe you nothing of the sort. The fact is, the old laws must be adhered to. This is simply a reckoning."

"This is simply bullshit," Forge shot back, and I mentally applauded his jab. "Either challenge me like a leader, or apologize, and we'll go home. I have other business to attend to."

You bet you do, buddy, I thought. *Like explaining what this Chosen bullshit all about.*

When the Elder did nothing but glower, Forge offered me his hand, and I dutifully took it, regretting I hadn't been much help. "Fine, then, we'll be off," he said.

"Sit down, Bastian." The Elder's voice vibrated with rage, the temperature in the room plunging to near-freezing in an instant. Phantom shadows swirled behind him, and the table in front of me began vibrating seconds before the air did. Suddenly, it was hard to breathe.

"Forge..." I said, his name turning into white mist.

"How do you propose we settle this bullshit, then?"

Forge asked, no hint of emotion in his voice. "Fight to the death, or do we come to another agreement?"

The Elder's eyes narrowed. "Death it is."

In my head, the vampires' voices rose in a chorus of bloodlust-fueled anticipation. It was difficult to single anyone out of the chaos, but after I sifted through them a second time, there was one voice that stood out. The Elder was finally speaking my language, and once I heard him, I wished I hadn't.

Forge wasn't here to settle a debt—he was simply standing in the Elder's way.

Meyer the Elder hadn't brought Forge here to settle an old score. He'd set this all up for...

"My champion." The Elder indicated the vampire stepping into the room with a casual wave. "I believe you two know each other."

This vampire was every bit as big as Forge, and bulkier, his arms bulging beneath the utilitarian blue coat. Everyone in the room broke the silence by talking at once, while I sized up the newcomer, doubt gnawing at me. He was huge, and his eyes glittered with something other than anticipation; they were full of anger. Around his neck was a thin white scar that he fingered while staring down Forge.

Cade. Even in my head, Forge bit the name off, as if it tasted sour. *Nobody to be concerned about.*

Really? Because he looks really scary.

Everyone here looks really scary, Selena. I have this under control, so don't panic.

Well, he really, really wants you dead. The rest of them are just here to watch. He's here to see that it gets done.

Selena.

Forge, you brought me here to listen. That's what I'm doing. And I'm telling you, you have to watch out for this guy.

Forge turned his gaze away from the Elder and fixed it on Cade, who returned it with a blackness that I hoped was never turned on me.

I snapped my shield firmly into place, relieved when Forge reinforced it with his, and watched the evil smile slowly disappear from the older vampire's face as Forge softly said, "It's been years, Cade. You don't look a day older than when we last met." Several vampires chuckled at what I supposed was standard vamp humor.

The Elder had reverted to his native language, but there was no mistaking his confidence. He'd set tonight up perfectly, and once Forge was out of the way, he'd get everything he wanted. And I wouldn't have time to explain, not while Forge and Cade were almost nose to nose.

"The only thing I care about is that after tonight, I will never think of you again," Cade said.

"Why do you think of me at all?" Forge asked softly. "Unless you still hold what happened to Mara against me."

"I would have protected her." Spittle flew out of Cade's mouth as he added, "Better than you."

"You would have died along with her." Forge shook his head sadly. "That's what this is all about? Some long-held grudge for something that happened so long ago it should have been forgotten?"

He stood, bracing his hands on the table so he stared straight at Cade, but his words were for all of them. "I killed the Elder's bastard. He murdered my Maker, and I invoked the right of blood to avenge her death. All of which was perfectly within the laws of Assembly. There's a good reason I've stayed in America all these years. You've never kept up with the times. Maybe it's time you let go of these outdated customs. Catch up; there's a whole new world out there."

Across the table, Cade imitated Forge's stance as his

huge hands clenched into fists. "Mara was mine long before she was yours."

"You lost her long before I came along."

While I was unraveling this puzzle of history between Cade and Forge, the Elder rapped his knuckles on the table. "The contest will occur tonight. There will be no opportunity for Bastian Forge to evade the sentence imposed by this Assembly." Instead of commanding, he sounded petulant, but maybe that was because Cade was sucking all the air out of the room at the moment.

Forge shrugged out of his jacket. "So be it. Where shall we do this? I expect you have my demise thoroughly planned out, *Meyer*." When his cold gaze slid around the table, most of the vampires shrank back, while others dropped their gazes to their laps. "Look at you all. So bloodthirsty, but at heart, you're nothing but a bunch of cowards." No one contradicted him.

"You and I, then," Cade growled as he slipped his coat off, revealing a defined, muscled body as ripped as Forge's.

I was having a hard time keeping my face composed, when my feelings were all over the place. I had to tell Forge what I'd discovered, but I couldn't afford to distract him from what was happening. Then there was the matter of keeping my shield in place, when all around me, I felt vampires poking at it, trying to worm their way inside to access my thoughts. I'd prepared to defend myself against one, maybe two vampires, not an entire table of them, and I was failing miserably.

Forge took off the cuff links, pressed them into my hands, then peeled off his shirt.

Holy hell.

Forge was hot. Like really, really hot. Like sizzling, melt-my-panties hot.

As I grappled with this new realization—and the sheer inappropriateness of it, given the circumstances—Cade stripped down until they were both naked to the waist. "Are we doing this in here?" Forge asked, scanning the well-appointed room. "Seems like a waste of good furniture."

"Outside," Cade snarled, showing huge fangs. The other vamps parted like the Red—black, actually—Sea as he shouldered roughly through them on his way out.

What about Dobson? I don't see him anywhere. He had men waiting...

Taking care of that right now.

I was taking Forge's advice and sticking close. But not too close, because whatever he was about to do, I wanted to be outside the range of it. It was a good thing I'd fallen back a pace.

Two heavily muscled vamps converged on Forge the second he passed through the exterior door, their scarred faces telling of a violent past. Cade paused to watch the fun and smirked as they caught Forge by the arms, one on each side, pummeling him with their free fists. The sound—hollow, meaty and deep—grossed me out on a primal level, but when I rushed forward to help, I was snatched off the ground by a set of viselike arms.

Struggling, I was dragged backward through the house, further and further away from Forge, and as I watched him disappear completely, my heart thudded against the pressure of the vampire's restraining arms. "*Forge,*" I screamed, my cry ringing through the house.

Kicking and twisting did me no good, but I managed to work an arm loose and elbow the asshole in the face. Blood spurted everywhere, and when his grip relaxed, I wiggled out away from him, blood dripping from my hair.

The vampire wiped his gushing nose and grinned at me

through the red smear across his face, my breaths coming fast as I backed away, my left hand blindly searching for any kind of weapon.

"*Forge,*" I yelled again, realizing how out of my element I was. So much for my grand plans to be a super spy and hold my own against another race. I couldn't find so much as a newspaper to defend myself with as the still-grinning bastard herded me toward the corner. *Dear God, please don't let me die being stupid.*

I'd just given up hope when a shadowy blur caught the vampire in the side, driving him across the room and into the fireplace. The huge mirror over the mantel tipped and burst into slivers as it hit the floor, raining glass all over us. Forge held my attacker to the wall, then, faster than I could see, swiped his hand across the other's neck. As blood spurted from his throat, Forge dropped his body to the floor.

"You're bleeding." He caught my face in his hand and tipped up my chin to get a good look.

"I..." Indeed, the dead vampire's blood was all over me, dripping from my hair to my destroyed dress. "It's not mine," I reassured him, hanging on to him for dear life, my gaze slipping all over the room, from the spreading blood to the shattered mirror, to the faces gaping in the doorway, to Forge. "I'm okay—it's his blood, not mine." I motioned to my now-deceased captor.

Forge took my hand, then whipped around to face the vampires congregating behind us.

"She is under my protection. Any one of you fuckers lay a finger on her, you'll end up right next to him." A nod at the dead vampire. "I claim blood rights on Cade." His lip inched up, revealing long white fangs. "And Dobson, that little fuck, if he hasn't turned tail and run."

"Cade is waiting out back," someone said quietly, and gave us a clear path to the door.

I was numb, having seen too much, too quickly, and struggled just to put one foot in front of the other. Forge, on the other hand, was on a mission, and I tried to match his long strides. When he set me beside one of the female vamps, I instinctually edged away from her.

"She's a friend," Forge murmured against my ear, pressing me back in place. "She'll protect you if this goes sideways." The woman motioned me closer, and I caught the glint of gold on her finger. A ring. An ouroboros ring.

I grabbed at him, but he was already gone. All I could do was watch the two of them circle each other like jackals. Physically, they were evenly matched, Forge making up for his lack of bulk with smooth, predatory movements. I just hoped he was as agile as he looked, because Cade looked... God, he looked deadly. His hand was as big as my entire head.

The other vampires closed in, but instead of anticipatory, their expressions were thoughtful, as if this contest was something they hadn't considered. I caught fragments of doubtful thoughts as they maneuvered around us for a better view.

"I think Cade made a terrible mistake tonight," the blonde beside me whispered, her words deeply accented. Or maybe it was from her fangs. "My guess is, Bastian will be reducing our numbers even further."

I hoped she was right with all my heart.

Never had I thought it would come to this.

Killing, now that I'd experienced it firsthand, was something I'd like to go the rest of my life without seeing. Especially all of this gruesome, dispassionate killing. Their voices drifted through my head, each of them looking to use this situation to their advantage. Even my blond bodyguard, whose sinfully sensual thoughts about Forge made jealousy swirl in the pit of my stomach.

But there was no doubt that Bastian was something to see, a lean whipcord of muscles and sinew, his expression ferocious, his fangs longer than anything I'd ever imagined coming out of someone's mouth. Damn, he was sexy. Sexier than I'd ever given him credit for, and now—seeing him like this—I wondered why, exactly, he'd been hiding this side of himself from me.

Because I liked this version of him.

Far more than I should.

17

I knew Selena was scared, and I hated not being able to reassure her that this final contest was all part of my plan. Even though I'd expected this, I'd have to use everything to beat Cade, since he was the deadliest fighter in our clan. As for Dobson, I'd run that little shit down once this contest was over and take him apart, piece by cowardly piece.

She'd stayed on top of the situation, though, warning me about the first attack. It was also apparent that she'd over-heard something else, but we'd have to go over that later. Right now, Cade was my concern.

Cade was a hundred years older than me. He'd been Mara's Maker—and lover—for a century by the time she decided she wanted me instead. He was the only other vampire in our clan who was strong enough to take me on, something I'd considered when deciding to face them all. He might be older than me, perhaps even bigger, but I was confident I'd end this. That confidence was the only reason I'd let Selena anywhere near the rest of these bloodsuckers.

Granted, I should have told Selena about Cade and

Mara and me from the beginning, but somehow...I hadn't found the opportunity to delve into my complicated past. Maybe I'd been hoping none of it would come up.

Cade vanished, moving so fast that the naked eye couldn't track him, but I didn't need to see Cade to kill him.

His signature move was to materialize directly behind his victim, then slit their throat before they even knew he existed. He'd done it often enough that it became predictable. The slightest rush of air on my left was all the warning I needed. My right hand shot out and connected with his chest, stopping him cold. In the second before Cade could recover, my other hand shot out and tore through his chest, leaving a long, bloody wound.

He vanished again, then materialized a few feet away, his expression murderous.

This time when he vanished there was no warning, only the red-hot slicing of a knife through my side, followed by the warm gush of blood. Selena screamed, then clapped a hand over her mouth, her eyes huge. Cade chuckled, gesturing toward her.

"I do love when my audience is receptive."

Her expression changed from horrified to thunderous, and she dropped her hand to reveal a perfectly blank face. Except for her narrowed eyes that brimmed with rage.

We crashed into each other, hands tearing flesh, teeth gnashing. Despite his size, I flipped Cade over, and he landed on his front, then pressed him against the dirt as he flailed and shouted. One hard strike against the back of his neck and blood splattered everywhere. He went still, his eyes going dim.

"Leave him for the sun," I ordered the rest of them, then went to find the Elder. I intended to ensure there'd be no repeat performance of tonight. He wanted to play by thousand-year-old rules, so be it. I'd do the same.

I slowed down when I drew even with Selena. "Stay here. I'll be back in a minute," I told her, and at my nod, the blonde gripped her arm so Selena did just that. I didn't want her anywhere near that old bastard. Not when I knew what he was capable of.

Her face screwed up. She wasn't happy, and I didn't blame her one bit, but I either handled this now, or it haunted us forever.

The Elder was still seated in the dining room, both guards stationed behind him, looking for all the world like a desiccated corpse.

"Cade's dead, and your little coup d'état is over. I met the conditions of our little blood match, which means you and I are *finished*. Clear enough?"

He looked me over like I was still a newborn. Smiling, I leaned closer, watching his guards out of the corner of my eye. I raised my hand to my mouth, then ran a fang along my palm. Blood bloomed, and I nodded for the Elder to do the same.

"You want to come after me again. I assure you, that would be a mistake. I have satisfied the rules you set down for this contest. You lost, and we are done. Believe me when I tell you that I won't play by your rules again."

His face sagged slightly, his eyes glinting with resentment as he sliced his palm open with a knife.

"You will stay away from me and mine. Forever." Our hands met, the blood making our handshake slippery. He was old, but his grip was strong, and I knew I'd be a fool to underestimate him. But a blood oath was a start.

"*Schan svu,*" he agreed.

I turned to go, then changed my mind.

"Something else. The girl is under my protection, and the protection of the Ouroboros Society. I am her Immortal Keeper, and if you dare..." I leaned closer, well aware I was covered with the blood of at least four vampires. "Touch her, I will kill you and take your place as Elder."

"*Tresset culde ment.*" *You can try.*

"If you think for one second I want your shitty little job in this backwards clan, you can think again. The world changed centuries ago, and you missed it."

I left him stewing in his own jealousy and went to collect Selena and take her home.

18

I didn't think I'd ever been so happy to set foot on a plane. Not that the feeling would last once we got into the air, but damn, I felt like I was barely escaping Scotland with my life.

"You did well, Selena."

"Yeah, well, you did too. All the random killing was a surprise. A little warning would have been nice." *Then I could have at least closed my eyes and not had all of that gruesomeness tattooed on my brain for the rest of my life.*

"I apologize for that."

He reached for my hand, but I drew it away. Violence wasn't what I'd signed up for. At least, not that much violence. "Of course you do," I snapped, not even sure why I was so pissed off as I buckled myself into my seat.

I'd kept my word, survived the vampire apocalypse and now we were on our way back home, my debt completely fulfilled. I should be ecstatic. I'd saved the company, and now all I had to do was bottle and release Dad's special batch and live out my life.

Instead, I was...mad.

I wasn't even sure why.

Sure, I was jealous. Jealous of Mara, and of the blonde who looked at Forge like she wanted to eat him up. But deep in the pit of my stomach, I knew there was more to it than that.

He'd withheld so much from me. Some of the omissions I understood, but others...

Why not warn me how dangerous this was? Why not tell me about Mara, about why he'd been targeted in the first place? Which led me to jump to all kinds of conclusions about what else he was hiding.

I mulled over Forge's many transgressions as my hand found the pendant and worried it up and down the chain, reminding me that Forge was hiding something even bigger from me. The Ouroboros Society. Chosen.

None of that made any sense to me, and I wasn't about to ask Forge to explain.

When I'd gone to him, it was to leverage his sense of loyalty to my family and help me save the company.

Now I had to ask myself, who was playing whom?

I'd gotten what I wanted, and kept my part of the bargain. My gaze drifted over to Forge, who was staring out the window. I thought I'd understood the dynamics between us. But for the first time, I wondered what it was that Forge really wanted out of this deal.

EVER SINCE SHE'D fastened her seatbelt, Selena had stopped hiding her thoughts behind a blank mask. I saw everything flicker across her face as easily as if I were watching a movie. She was angry with me. She distrusted me. She even feared me, if the sharp tang of adrenaline in the cabin was anything to go by.

I could guess why—not that I had the ability to change the past.

"When we get back, I want us to sit down and talk," I told her, pulling her out of her thoughts. "There are many things I have to tell you, some that I should have told you before Assembly."

Her eyes flickered with surprise, then shuttered closed, as suspicion oozed from her. I swore her lip curled, then she settled that damnable mask down over her face.

"Selena."

She turned her head robotically—obediently—toward me, and I suppressed my curse. *I should have been honest with her from the beginning.*

If you had, she would have run as far away from you as she could get.

"I know you have questions after what happened tonight. When we get home, I will tell you whatever you want to know."

No reaction, not even so much as a nod.

To her credit, she'd kept her shield firmly in place, and her lack of trust gutted me. Again, I forced down a curse, and the anger that only reminded me this was my fault. Honesty was not something I was familiar with, since I mostly dealt with my own kind. Part of me had forgotten that when I made my proposal.

"I'm sorry you were frightened. I'm sorry for what you had to see tonight."

I couldn't read her face, nor her thoughts. I was so used to reading everyone around me, and this silence was maddening.

"Don't shut me out, Selena," I said gently. But she

already had, and I was damned if I knew how to get through.

She turned her face fully toward me, and I winced at the blood, the tangled hair, the beginnings of a bruise on her face.

"There's a bathroom, back there." I motioned toward the rear of the plane, keeping my eyes on that bruise. "Towels, anything you need will be in there. Take your time." I handed her the bag she'd brought on board. She looked surprised before she took it from me.

Without a word, she unbuckled her belt, walked to the rear cabin and locked herself inside.

From where I sat, it looked like we'd both gotten exactly what we wanted, and neither of us were happy.

19

I shut the door then locked it, knowing that the flimsy barrier would pose no obstacle to Forge if he decided he wanted to get through. After looking around the bedroom—Forge's bedroom—I sank into the nearest chair, burying my face in my hands.

I didn't know how I was supposed to feel about what I'd seen tonight. Didn't know if I was *capable* of feeling, since I only felt numb.

At the moment, I hated Forge, but he was right. I had to get cleaned up.

There was something oddly sensual about showering in Forge's shower, and I sat back in the chair to get dressed, since sitting on Forge's enormous bed seemed way too intimate. I wanted to put as much distance between me and him right now, if for no other reason than to sort everything out for myself. Death and vampires and a secret society that I, apparently, was a member of.

Inspecting myself in the foggy mirror, I concluded that at least I wasn't all bloody, and that was about as optimistic as I dared to be. My clothes were clean, but wrinkled, my hair was dripping wet, and yes, there would definitely be a bruise on my cheek tomorrow. This was not how I'd expected this trip to end.

I'd had grand plans for Scotland, just like I did with everything in life, and ending up further embroiled in Forge's life hadn't been part of it. I'd done this to save the company, and in that, at least, I'd accomplished my goal. Extricating myself from what was looking more and more like a trap would be harder.

A gentle rap on the door, and I paused as Forge asked, "Do you need anything, Selena?"

"No. I'm good." I was pissed I had to answer at all. I'd intended the flight back to Philly to be silent. At least on my part. I threw tonight's ruined clothing into the trash and zipped my bag closed. Sitting out there with Forge for six hours was a daunting proposal, but I could certainly keep *my* mouth shut until we landed in Philadelphia. Then I'd never have to see him again.

I pressed my ear to the door and didn't hear anything, so I eased it open and found Forge on his cell with his back to me. I chose a seat by the window, as far from him as I could get, and plugged in my music then jammed the earphones into my ears. Instantly, the even hum of the plane was eclipsed by reggae.

Forge made no move to engage me, instead making a series of calls that seemed to last forever. Watching Forge out of the corner of my eye proved difficult at best, and at some point, my head bobbing to Peter Tosh, I fell asleep.

The next thing I knew, I was lifted up and carried, my face pressed into Forge's chest. For a second, I breathed in his cologne before I remembered to be mad at him.

"Put me down," I demanded, although there was little heat in the order. My mind was foggy, full of competing images—*Forge tearing a heart out of a chest, Forge holding me like I was the most precious thing in the world*—that I was trying to sort out, while my heart engaged in a similar tug of war.

"In a moment, Selena," he said, his face turned toward something ahead of us. I twisted just in time for him to set me into the back of a long, dark limo. I pressed my bag into my side, getting my bearings as Forge slid in beside me.

"Take me home," I told him, not wanting to spend another second with him. "Four-seventy-three Brookline Road."

Forge rapped on the window. "Take us home. No stops." The car sped up slightly and made a turn, heading away from the city.

"We're going the wrong way. I want to go home, Forge," I insisted, folding my hands in my lap. Mostly so I wouldn't slap him in the face. "*My home*, in case I wasn't clear."

"You will. Once you and I have hashed this out between us."

"Hash what out, exactly? I kept my word, and you bailed out the company. You lied to me about pretty much everything in the process, but who am I to judge? Maybe that's how you do things in *your world*." My emotions were swinging wildly all over the place, from hurt to betrayal to general anger. "As far as I'm concerned, things between us are over."

"They're hardly over." A grim smile twisted his mouth, one that I couldn't quite decipher, and my heart sank, as it looked like he meant to have his way. "Aren't you even a little bit curious about what happened tonight? I'd like a chance to explain, but only if you're willing to give it to me."

Just like the bastard to back me into a corner, betting on my sense of fair play.

"One hour," I said. "One hour and then we part ways."

I was still staring out the window as he answered, "Whatever you want, Selena."

20

W hen we arrived at Forge's newly transformed mansion, I felt a bite of fear as the car rolled up to the front doors. Several things had occurred to me during our ride here, and call it paranoia or an overactive imagination, but none of them were good. I could be a loose end as far as Forge was concerned, especially now that I'd seen the unbridled violence he was capable of.

What if you're nothing but a complication? It sounded ridiculous, even to my overly suspicious self, but after tonight, I wasn't discounting anything, no matter how wild.

I also knew I'd never be rid of Forge until he had his say. Not that I cared what he said, since obviously his track record spoke for itself.

"Come, Selena." He offered me his hand—now pristinely clean and manicured—and I ignored it, getting out on my own and stepping past him. No matter what he said, or how he said it, I was walking back through these doors in an hour, with my hands washed of Mr. Bastian Forge forever.

There was a fire going in the library and a pot of tea and sandwiches set out on the enormous desk. I didn't know who'd put them there—magic, maybe—but they smelled delicious. I helped myself to a sandwich and dragged a small chair closer to the fire, figuring that would put enough room between me and Forge, and me one step closer to the door.

"I want to apologize—"

"Let's skip past your second attempt at an apology and fast-forward to the part where you explain how Scotland turned into a blood-fest. That's something I would have liked a heads-up on before I boarded the plane."

When his lips tightened, I half regretted the way I was acting, but then I remembered all the things he'd withheld from me and notched my chin higher.

"I should have," Forge said. "I withheld information from you because I knew the truth would spook you. While you thought you knew me from stories you'd heard, there is no way to prepare a human for the level of violence that exists in my world."

I finished my sandwich and looked longingly at the plate across the library. "You could have at least tried, Forge. What would have been worse? Me having some idea of what was coming, or to be completely blindsided?"

"I agree." He lowered his head. "I should have trusted you. I should have allowed you to make the decision. I didn't know whether I could trust you yet."

"Now look where we are," I grumbled, finally crossing the room for another sandwich. "I don't trust you anymore," I told him flatly, then watched his face as I nibbled away at the crust. "To be honest, I don't know if I ever can."

Instead of looking guilty, he looked eager, his face showing a trace of anticipation. "I said you could ask me anything," he reminded me. "I meant it. What do you want to know?"

My list would take all night, but I settled for the one thing that was still a complete mystery to me, yet seemed to take precedence in the *Forge is a total liar* department.

"What is a Chosen, and who appointed *you* my... What did you call yourself? My Immortal Keeper?"

His eyes widened slightly, and he rose to stoke the fire.

He's already thinking of a way around it, to explain it away. I checked my phone. Forty minutes to go, and I wouldn't even look back.

"The Ouroboros Society is very old, and not exactly in the public eye. We have nothing that holds us together except for our philosophy. We believe in nurturing and developing special abilities in humans. Anyone from a skilled cellist to a stem-cell researcher—when we come across a deserving human, we protect them. We teach them, whenever possible."

"Which means you only agreed to help me because I had an ability you wanted to exploit."

"No more than you wanted to exploit my friendship with Ambrose to get what *you* wanted."

Stalemate on that one. While on the surface, Forge had my motives right, there were a hundred other reasons I'd gone to him, and would probably—given the circumstances— make the same choice again. Not that I was proud of what I'd done, but nor had I *lied about everything.*

"What, exactly, is a Chosen?" I lifted the pendant. "Do we all wear one of these?"

"Yes, all Chosen wear the pendant." He turned away from the fire and walked to the desk, giving me a wide berth. He pulled something out of his pocket and set it on the table, the gold glinting in the firelight. "Patrons wear something similar. It's usually quite subtle—these cuff links, for instance—but the jewelry will always have the symbol on it."

"You're like my...patron?" That term sounded almost benign, nor did it mean the same thing as "keeper." Maybe I'd gotten the wrong impression from Forge's over-the-top reaction, when he'd practically claimed me as his in front of the others.

He put his hand over his heart and gave me a half-bow. "At your service."

I ignored him, but it was becoming harder to keep my hatred burning bright.

"Does this make things dangerous for me in any way?" I remembered how the Elder had looked at me, as if he couldn't wait to sink his claws into me, and how Dobson had leered at me.

"An enemy would recognize it, yes. But allies will also protect you if they know you are Chosen. All the members don't know each other, but that symbol unites us in purpose."

"My abilities." I veered off onto a wild tangent: "Are they from Ambrose, or are they completely random?" I held my breath as Forge considered this.

"No. Ambrose had a way about him, but wasn't blessed with your specific ability. His gift was knowing what someone was thinking—but it was only a feeling, he said, not the capability to read thoughts word for word, as you do. He and I certainly never communicated mentally. Still, his intuition came in handy when we arrived in the new world."

"Why don't all vampires employ someone with this kind of ability, then? I'd think they'd all have someone who can read minds by their side, if only to even the odds."

"Your kind is so rare that most of my people have never

seen your like. Most vampires despise humans, and so, would never form an alliance with them. They think of your kind only as sport and food." Forge shot me a pointed look. "Especially the vampires who attended Assembly."

If he thought he was being forthcoming, he was wrong. This was even more reason for me to be mad at him for withholding the truth and letting me walk into a freaking bloodbath.

"Some of us, though, are intrigued by humans. The society is proof of that." He rubbed his hands up and down his thighs. "I know you don't trust me, Selena, and you have good reason. I should have been more honest with you, but I haven't interacted with humans in a very long time. The only reason I agreed... I was intrigued by a woman who would break a two-hundred-year-old agreement. Once I discovered you could read my thoughts, all I thought of was how I could use you to give me an advantage over the Elder."

"Finally," I muttered. "The truth."

"I'd like to hear it come out of your mouth, for once, since I'm the only one laying everything out on the table. You manipulated me as well to get what you wanted." Forge sounded testy, and my temper rose a notch, too, as I picked up on the slight vibration in his voice. "You could admit it."

I could. I just didn't want to.

My hand strayed to the necklace, and I began worrying the pendant along the chain. I would have torn the thing from my neck had Forge not reminded me, sternly enough that I knew he was serious, to never take it off.

"Could it be genetic?" I asked instead, with no intention of admitting to anything. "Were there any Langstons in between me and Ambrose who had special abilities?"

"I wouldn't know, because all the other Langstons followed directions and stayed away from me."

Well, okay, valid point. "Still. Can this be a genetic trait of some kind? I find it hard to believe my ability's a random fluke."

"I don't think that either, Selena."

We sat in silence for a minute, having finally come to an agreement over something.

"This ability of mine..." I was getting paranoid now. "Would it be valuable to any other vampire? One who might want to use me like you did?" *Use* being a rather loose term for feeding me, training me and taking me to Scotland. Oh, and saving the company that I loved in the process.

However, it was the wrong word, because Forge's face grew pinched. I thought I saw a shadow darken his skin, but then it passed, and his expression grew clear again.

"You would be targeted, *if* a vampire knew for certain what you were," he admitted, and my nervousness faded somewhat.

The reflection of flames flickered in his dark eyes, while the gold light threw his face into sharp contrast. He looked tired, not bothering to watch me expectantly anymore. He was withdrawing from me, turning into the Forge I'd met that first night. It was obvious this conversation wasn't going the way he wanted, either.

I totally understood how he felt when he added, "Now that the Elder has seen you, there's no doubt he'll be curious." He shoved his hands into his pockets, and didn't sound any happier than me when he added, "Which is why you'll be staying with me for the time being."

HOURS LATER, I was still trying to explain it to him. "I can't stay here, Forge," I said, for what felt like the hundredth time. "I have a life. I have to go to work."

If it was possible, his face was darker than I'd ever seen it. He'd given up arguing with me an hour ago, so now I was basically explaining over and over why I couldn't possibly live here with him while he glowered at me.

For the freaking hundredth time.

"Have the car brought around—or whatever—and take me home." I had my bag in a death grip and was seriously frustrated. "Let me out of here, Forge."

If I didn't see the faint rise and fall of his chest, I would have thought he was a statue. One minute he was unmoving, the next, he was right beside me, hand wrapped around my arm.

With those unsettling eyes boring into mine, he asked, "What will you do if the Elder comes after you?"

My lower lip snuck between my teeth before I settled my face so Forge couldn't read my emotions. Not that he'd be able to, since my emotions were all over the place right now. Forge was offering me safety, but safety with Forge presented several problems. Not the least of which was that I wasn't looking at Forge like a mentor or a patron or even a friend. Somewhere around that table filled with vampires, he'd become something more.

Somehow, that scared me more than facing the Elder on my own.

"I'll be fine," I said, feeling anything but. "You won, right? It's over?"

"If he does come after you, Selena, there will be casualties. In fact, the Elder enjoys killing more than is natural, even for a vampire. People could get hurt. People you love." His eyes softened. "Stay here. Let me keep you safe."

"Way to lay on the emotional blackmail, and a slightly over-the-top warning, Forge." I sighed. "Okay, you're right. I don't want anyone to get hurt on my behalf. But even if I do stay here, the distillery is non-negotiable. I have to go in and work. Even though you bailed us out, there are still things to take care of, and we have to get ready to make the next batch."

His warm eyes and his speech about keeping me safe were doing weird things to my insides. Getting my way on work would at least mean I didn't have to be around him twenty-four seven.

He inclined his head. "That is acceptable."

And that was how Forge and I became roommates.

The tightness in my chest loosened as Selena agreed to stay here, where I could protect her. While I doubted the Elder would personally attack me, since we'd enacted the blood oath, he'd been looking too closely at Selena. I didn't trust that bastard, nor the rest of my power-hungry clan. They were too ruthless for me to turn my back on, which was why I had to keep her with me.

But most importantly, I had to win back her trust. I'd broken it, but I hoped having her here would give me time to do just that. To prove to her I was not only honorable, but she could rely on me without question.

"I'll show you to your room," I said. Temper flared in her eyes, then flickered out just as quickly. She was tired, confused and angry. I wasn't thinking too clearly myself. Right now, she was my only concern, but I didn't know how to wipe away the past twenty-four hours.

I didn't know if I wanted to. Having her see me in my most natural state—however violent—had satisfied the most male part of me. When I'd transformed in the car, there had been a definite flicker of interest in her eyes, as well as a burst of heat.

The faint brush of her lips against mine had ignited something primitive inside of me, something that was getting stronger by the hour.

I gestured to her door, realizing too late that I hadn't said a word the entire way up here. She waited indecisively, looking between me and the door, so I pushed it open. This room had been unused, but it was on the same wing as mine, in case the Elder—or anyone else—got through my security.

I wasn't going to spook Selena by telling her that, but then I changed my mind. Concealment and lies had gotten us nowhere, so it was time to change tactics. "I'm on this wing as well," I said. She drew in a breath, as if she was going to argue, but stopped herself. "If anyone attempts to hurt you, I'm right next door," I explained, even though this wasn't the real reason I wanted her close. "The other wing of the house is in some disrepair, as it hasn't been open for a long time. I managed to get this room renovated in time for our return."

"You knew we'd return?" she said, shaking her head. "I wasn't sure that was a given."

"Have a little faith in me, Selena. I won't allow anything to happen to you."

She gave me a quizzical look before she drifted into the room, holding her bag tightly. The room was adequately prepared, light and clean, which was all that was necessary. I suddenly wished the carpets were deeper, and the comforter warmer as she ran her fingers over everything while circling the room slowly.

"This is beautiful." I barely caught the words, muttered as they were, but the look on her face was reverent. "You got this ready for me? Knowing we'd be back?"

"Of course," I said impatiently. "While I hoped your abilities would escape the Elder's detection, I also prepared for the possibility he'd discern what you were." I gestured to a pile of boxes and the clothes over the chair. "I took the liberty of having some of your belongings brought over."

That brought a sour look to her face, and she gave me the evil eye, but the Elder may have someone watching her house, and eliminating all possible threats took preplanning. I didn't have time to ask permission.

"Let's talk terms," Selena said, bouncing nervously on the edge of the bed. "So there's no confusion."

"Such as?" I knew what her terms were going to be, but for once, Selena was not going to get her way. Not entirely.

"I drive myself to and from the distillery every single day. I can go anywhere on the property, and I stay until I'm done." By the end, her head had taken on a stubborn tilt, her eyes flashing.

I nodded. "We will make that work."

She blinked and stroked the blanket beneath her, clearly unsure how to handle things after I'd agreed so readily. Her safety was important, but so was her happiness. Cooping her up would do no one any good, and she'd only resent me more than she already did. If we were to make any progress, she had to trust me. Which meant I had to tell her the truth.

"Of course, it occurred to me I've been an absentee partner." I smiled at her, and her eyes went straight to my fangs. "An oversight I mean to correct. Which means you can spend tomorrow showing me around the distillery."

I suppressed my chuckle at the look of horror that came over her face.

"Including my office, since, from now on, we'll be working closely together, Miss Langston."

22

Any other time, sleeping in a gorgeous room outfitted with exquisite antiques and super-plush bedding would have thrilled me. There was something decadent about silky, clean sheets that I just loved.

But tonight, it was all I could do to sort through the clothes he'd had brought over, setting aside work clothes versus casual clothes. A baggy sweatshirt in my hand, I stood there for a minute, wondering what Forge and I would ever do that was casual, finally deciding to cross that bridge another time.

Sleep eluded me, as I spent most of the night stewing, dropping my shield and hoping Forge heard *every single word.* He'd been pulling the strings all along, and it irked me. He'd lied to me, then proceeded to manipulate me *yet again* into staying. Now I was fuming, and replaying everything in my head over and over. Whatever temporary fondness I'd developed for Forge was long gone.

When my alarm dinged, I rubbed the sand from my eyes and stumbled to the bathroom, praying there were clean towels. I needn't have bothered. Forge had everything set out, toiletries—the extravagant sort I'd never buy—mirrors, brushes and a dizzying assortment of makeup and lotions. As if he didn't know what to get, so he just bought everything at the store.

Best of all was the stack of fluffy towels.

I gathered my dripping hair into a band, ruing the fact it would be huge by lunchtime, a big, blond, bushy mess on top of my head. But I didn't have time to blow-dry it and get to the distillery on time. Emerson had already called three times this morning, and I'd let them all go to voicemail. I didn't know what to say to him right now, when I still had Forge to deal with this morning.

Forge and his crazy notion to go to work with me.

I tugged my collar into place, then slipped the pendant beneath my shirt. All anyone could see was the chain, which was...a good thing? Since enemies and allies would look the same to me, concealing it made the most sense. At least until I figured out the rules.

I was headed for the front door, no intention at all of gathering up Forge, when the rustle of paper stopped me in my tracks.

"Good morning, Miss Langston."

My mouth went dry. Like middle-of-the-desert dry.

He was dressed in a sleek, dark blue suit, the slight stretch of the wool accentuating the width of his shoulders. When he set the paper aside and rose, it was as if he was a flag unfurling, the white shirt and bright red tie complementing his paleness, the dark hair and eyes. In short, Bastian Forge in a suit was devastating.

"You were serious," I said, wondering how this would go over in a company where he'd become something of a legend. People would certainly have something to talk about today.

"Deadly serious, Miss Langston."

"Forge..."

"Mr. Forge, if you please," he said, his voice pleasant, almost playful. "We will be working together, and I assume familiarity in the workplace is still frowned upon?"

"Okay, I agree. If we're going to do this, Miss Langston and Mr. Forge will work."

"Oh, this will work."

I did a double take. Was Forge making a joke?

Then all I saw was the brand-new Land Rover as it rolled up to the door. The driver and Forge exchanged a few words, then Forge climbed into the passenger seat and looked at me expectantly. Cursing, I made my way to the driver's side.

"Where is my car, Forge?"

"Mr. Forge," he corrected me.

"When I said I would drive myself to work," I said, holding the wheel in a death grip, "I meant *my* car. Not this"—I looked at the dashboard, completely thrown off my snark game—"marvel of technology," I finished lamely, noting the speedometer went up to one hundred and fifty. Yes, I would drive Forge's manipulative ass to work today and see what kind of a backseat driver he was.

Twenty minutes later—record time—we pulled into the employee parking lot at Langston-Forge. The lot behind warehouse number four, and somewhere beneath the gravel was the old asphalt, but I still had the same parking spot I'd used since I turned sixteen and started coming to work.

The tires slid before grabbing, and it was totally worth almost hitting the chain-link fence just to see a flash of dismay cross Forge's face as I skidded to a stop, right in the center of my spot.

That expression might just be worth driving him to work every day.

"We're here," I said brightly as he glowered at me. "Have a great first day at work, darling."

I'd totally meant it as a joke, but something cut through his scowl when I said it. Almost a look of pleasure, which I totally ignored. I'd really have to watch my snark game around Forge, which was definitely going to be hard, if not impossible. Feeling somewhat better, I slammed my door and headed for the main building.

"We can begin the day by you showing me to my office, Miss Langston."

I should have known I wasn't going to shake him that easily, but surely he wasn't planning to stick with me *all* day? We did a quick circuit of the warehouses, since they were the closest, then headed back to the main building.

"I remember when Ambrose built this building," Forge...*Mr. Forge*...murmured as I set my hand on the heavy outside door to push it open.

"That's the sort of thing you're going to want to keep to yourself," I told him. "Otherwise, you're in for an interesting day." We wound through the main floor, then down the steps to the basement, knots of employees gathering in our wake, the whispers deafening. "I'll have the office across from me cleaned out for you today. That way you can get set up." I had no idea what, if anything, Forge was going to set up, but if he had his own space, then maybe he wouldn't be hovering around me all day.

We'd almost made it to my office when Emerson Holloway stepped through my door into the hallway. I made a mental note to have him give me poker lessons, as a faint look of surprise wrinkled his forehead before he quickly smoothed his face out and offered his hand to Forge.

"Mr. Forge. A pleasure. Is Selena showing you around today?"

Emerson always struck the perfect balance. Polite, yet requiring an answer.

"She is." Forge's gaze seemed to fall on everything at once. Me, Holloway, the office he'd exited from. "I've decided to take a more active role in the company."

Now Emerson didn't bother to hide his surprise. "Is that so?" Only I heard the slightly bitter note undercutting his politeness. "We will need to notify the board." His gaze cut to me. I could already hear him warning me again about taking the money from Forge. But neither could I explain to Emerson why, exactly, Forge was here. Nor my newly discovered abilities. Not if I wanted to continue running this company. If my near-dismissal from the board had taught me one thing, it was that appearances counted.

Since both my sex and my youth counted against me already, I couldn't afford anyone to doubt my sanity.

"Mr. Forge expressed interest in learning the whisky business," I explained. "As he was gracious enough to bail the company out when we most needed it, I thought I should return the favor and show him what we do here."

Emerson was looking at me like he'd never seen me before.

"Besides, his name is on the building. Are you really going to tell him no?"

"Of course not," Emerson immediately replied. "It's just a shock, after all this time. Selena's right, of course. Make yourself at home and let her show you around. She knows more about this place than anyone else."

The day spun by at a dizzying speed. Even though I had

piles of backlogged work to catch up on, Forge expected me to show him everything along the way. Between his curiosity and my three-day absence, it was almost seven before I realized how exhausted I was.

Of course, had I actually slept last night, things would have been different, but I swayed slightly on my feet as I took Forge's picture down off my wall. It was my final task of the day, since it seemed beyond weird to have it hanging in here, while the vampire himself was in an office right across the hall. I would have taken it down first thing, but he'd already seen it. Awkward.

I pushed it behind the file cabinets before I pulled my door closed for the night. Forge was waiting outside in the hall, staying a few steps behind me as we wound our way through the old building, then outside.

"It's interesting," Forge said as we made our way between two of the warehouses toward the parking lot. "You haven't really changed anything in the main building."

"We moved the offices to the basement to make space for a conference room, and a tasting room for tourists, of course. There's been talk of expanding that, but yeah, it's pretty much the same as when Ambrose built it. A few new roofs and modern upgrades, but it's served us well for years." I unlocked the vehicle, shuddering at how much it must have cost, and climbed in.

When Forge was buckled in beside me, he commented, "It felt good to be back there." I thought I detected a note of regret in that statement.

"Your distillery in Scotland. How long had it been since you'd visited?"

"Quite a few years. I hardly even recognized the driver, it had been that long. But it felt good. As if I'd gone home, if only for a short time."

"You meant what you said about staying in America?"

"I did." He shook his head. "It's a balancing act, staying alive in my world. One of the best ways to ensure a long life as a vampire is to put as much distance between yourself and other vampires as you can."

While that didn't seem like a solid long-term plan, I kept my mouth shut. I didn't know anything about vampires, anyway.

"When the telephone was invented, it became significantly easier to communicate. And now..." He brandished his cell phone. "Push of a button, and it's almost like being there."

"But not really." I backed out of the spot, skirting a large delivery truck coming in.

"No, not really. But it's the best I can hope for, given the circumstances."

"What would it take for you to go back? Permanently?"

"Trying to get rid of me so soon, Miss Langston?"

"Not trying at all. I'm just curious. The dynamics between everyone at the meeting...they were very similar to human interactions." *Without all the blood and gore.* "It stands to reason you'd like to return to Scotland, and something is preventing that. What would it take for you to go home?"

"The Elder would have to die and the rest of the clan would have to swear loyalty to me, which I don't want. Which means my return will never happen."

"Why not? You'd be a better leader than that desiccated old fool."

Forge smiled faintly. "I'll tell you the same thing I told him. I don't want it. I don't want any part of the shitshow that is my old clan. They live by antiquated rules. Rules I'd be obligated to enforce, if I were in charge. No thank you.

Besides, the Elder will never forget. Not that I killed his offspring, nor that I escaped his judgment."

God, and I thought humans knew how to hold a grudge. I couldn't imagine how long vampires could. Probably forever.

"Let's say he drops dead." Did vampires ever die? "I'll bet you'd go back in a heartbeat."

"Once, I would have. Now, I'm not sure. The distillery runs fine without me, and I've grown used to the modern comforts of my life here. What about you?"

"What about me?"

"Have you ever thought about leaving home?"

It felt odd to entertain the question. We were once again veering off into personal, forbidden territory. Territory that I had to immediately navigate away from. "I haven't thought much about it. Philly is my home, and I'm not ready to leave, not until I do everything I want to do."

"Do you know why Ambrose and I came to America together?"

"No."

"Because we were friends, and friends stick together." He leaned against the headrest as he closed his eyes. "Sometimes I forget what it was like to have someone you could trust. It's been a long time since I felt like that about anyone."

I kept my hands at two and ten and tried to explain away all the emotions racing through me right now. My heart was *not* hurting right now. And I definitely didn't want to pull over and pull him into my arms.

Unguarded Forge was dangerous. But I longed to hear more.

"But today, the second I set foot in the building, it all

came back to me. There's only been two humans I trusted. One was Ambrose, and the other is you."

Not knowing how to respond, I kept quiet, wondering why Forge was opening up all of a sudden. Before I knew it, we were cresting the hill at the top of the drive. I parked in front of the door, pocketing the keys on the way out. Forge followed me to the door, and for just a second, I had the strangest déjà vu that we were just your average, everyday couple coming home from work. Why I was thinking of us a couple, I didn't know, but there it was.

The warm, fuzzy feeling engulfed my stomach, then sank lower, smoldering in my core, while Forge pushed open the door for me. The place smelled clean—wax and cinnamon and lemons—and I toed off my shoes at the door.

Forge was practically crowding me as I dropped my briefcase into the nearest chair, wondering why this place was starting to feel like home.

23

T he second Selena and I breached the door, I knew something was wrong. Beneath the heavy smell of cleaners lurked a stranger's scent. Dobson.

Rage crackled in me at the thought of someone in my den, along with a prickle of doubt. How had the bastard gotten in? How did he know when we'd arrive?

I didn't leave Selena's side as she took off her shoes and set her bag down. I didn't hear him moving, but Dobson's scent was fresh, which meant he was nearby, waiting for his chance to take Selena.

With Selena's ability now exposed, she was a valuable commodity, one I knew the Elder would exploit fully. It was my job to protect her and keep the bastard from getting anywhere close to her.

There's someone in the house.

Beside me, she went completely rigid. *Who? Can you tell?*

I hesitated, but since we'd settled on the truth in most situations, I thought back to her, *Dobson.*

Even though I'd known a kidnapping attempt was possible, I was disappointed they'd jumped right into it. A little bit of loyalty among my own kind shouldn't be too much to ask for. Apparently, Dobson was willing to do anything, so long as the money was right. Which was predictable, as far as Dobson went. He'd always been a sketchy git.

Stay beside me. And keep your eyes closed.

While she obeyed, I sent my shadows out to find the intruder. They flew up the winding stairs, then down the hallway toward where our bedrooms were, and a moment later, I heard the scuffle of feet against the wood floor. The methodical thuds told me they were dragging him down to me, and as soon as the sound stopped, Dobson materialized in front of me, his arms bound tightly to his sides by my shadows.

My years in America had not only been spent avoiding my kind. I'd spent the time teaching myself—as the humans said—new tricks. This was one of them. Handy, when I couldn't leave Selena's side.

"I didn't invite you, Dobson," I told him civilly. "But I'm glad you're here. Maybe you can clear a few things up for me."

In response, the pale vampire hissed, as my shadows squeezed tighter. Selena was keeping close, as intrigued as she was scared. Her eyes were also open, blinking as she took in the sight before us. I would have—should have—explained this strange talent of mine, but I hadn't thought the situation would arise where she'd see it.

Ask him who sent him.

Obviously, that will be my first question.

"Why are you here, Dobson? Didn't my actions at Assembly deter you from trying to kidnap my Chosen?" The more the asshole fought against the shadows, the tighter they constricted. "You came here to harm Selena."

"I came because she is very valuable, Bastian." He licked

his lips. "She's worth a lot of money. Money I'd be willing to split with you."

The sound of my given name on that POS's tongue irked me, but not as much as his offer.

"We can share the reward from the Elder—trust me, it's more than generous. Once we hand her over to him, we'll divide it...half and half." The expectant expression on his face faded when he saw mine. "Okay, forty-sixty."

"Clearly, I don't need your money." I indicated the house around us. "Nor the Elder's. You've trespassed. You coordinated an attack on us in Edinburgh. But worst of all, Dobson, you came after her." My last word was nothing more than a low, feral growl, and Dobson's teeth punched out of his mouth.

I wasn't worried about Dobson escaping. I was worried about Selena and whether she wanted to see any more of this. Probably not.

"Selena, go to the library and lock the door," I told her, praying she'd obey with no argument. "Don't open it for anyone."

Except you.

Yes. Except for me.

She eyed the situation again before heading down the hallway. When I heard the distinctive click of the library's lock, I let my fangs descend as I decided where to strike first.

"I wouldn't have hurt her, Bastian, I swear. I was only going to take her to him, that's all, nothing more, and I was supposed to get her there in one piece. I only got involved because the Elder called in a favor. I didn't want any part of this. I was minding my own business..."

I looked on in disgust as Dobson went to his knees, begging for mercy.

"No one will ever take her away from me," I assured him. "Not you. Not the Elder, not the whole goddamn Assembly."

AFTER LOCKING the door tightly behind me, I doubled-checked the latch, just to make sure it was secure. I wasn't sure if I felt safer in here or outside with Forge. I'd known I'd see Dobson again; I just didn't think it would be this soon.

Then there were the shadowy things that seemed to leak out of Forge's fingers. I definitely wasn't going to think about *that*. I plunked down in the deep leather chair, warm from being so close to the fire, and realized I was shivering. No, I was *shaking*, as my teeth chattered loud enough to be heard.

Hi, my name is Forge. I'm a gazillionaire, and I can shoot shadows out of my hands. I like blood, mayhem and long walks on the beach.

The more I thought about what was happening outside the door, the more I began looking at the library's dark corners as a threat. Dobson had found me. Which meant the Elder likely knew where I was. Maybe he was on his way right now.

A muted scream echoed dully behind the door, and I sank down further into the chair.

I *hated* all of this violence.

Or did I?

Right now, I was more than happy Forge was out there dealing with Dobson, even though I knew what the outcome would be. I was grateful he'd been with me tonight. Glad I'd given in to his seemingly ridiculous demand and wasn't alone in *my* house, trying to outsmart Dobson.

No, when it suited me, I was okay with Forge's violence.

As if they heard me, there was a deep roar, a cut-off scream, a heavy thump and then silence.

I stayed put. No telling what was going on out there, and I didn't want to be part of it. Not yet, anyway. I might be okay with Forge's end result, but his methods were nothing I had to see in person. Knowing he was watching out for me was enough.

I waited for what seemed like forever, before Forge softly knocked on the door. "Selena?"

I ran to unlock it, wondering why, exactly, I was running, and then I inhaled Forge's rich scent as he caught me in his arms. It was one of those magical, movie-star moments, until it wasn't, as I head-butted him square in the nose.

"Oof," he grunted. Since I smashed up against him, I felt his breath go out in a whoosh.

I slid out of his arms and down his body as both of his hands went to his nose. "Shit, that fucking hurt. I'm bleeding." So much blood was pouring between his fingers that I left him and ran down the hall to get a towel from the kitchen.

By the time I got back, Forge had already stopped bleeding and I was left holding a handful of towels. "Ultra-fast coagulation," he explained, although the front of his shirt was soaked. He saw my eyes stray to the stain, and chuckled. "Don't worry; that's not mine. It's Dobson's."

Okay, the suspense was killing me. "Is he..." *Dead? Half-dead? Alive?*

"He'll never bother you again." Hearing the firm assurance in Forge's voice made that panicky, restless feeling fade. "What I don't know is how he gained access to the house in the first place. Or how he knew our schedule."

The squeamish feeling rushed right back through me.

"He knew when we'd be home," Forge pointed out pragmatically while my mind was scrambling around trying to figure out if I was happy that Dobson was dead. Jury was still out, although I was warming up to the idea.

"Maybe he followed us home?"

"Doubtful," Forge said, striding to the computer. "I upgraded the security this past week. Cameras throughout the property, including the road." He clicked the mouse, then a few keys and a grid of camera views came up on the screen. "I'll run this back, until... Ah, there you are, you little pissant."

I didn't know what Forge was looking at, because I couldn't see a thing except trees and darkness.

"I'll slow it down for you." He hit a button, and all of a sudden, Dobson materialized out of thin air, just like he had moments ago. "We move too quickly for a human to see. He beat us home by a few minutes."

I watched the Range Rover come up the drive, then stop at the front door. That sick feeling crept through me again as I watched myself get out, acting like I didn't have a care in the world.

"How do you know he just didn't follow us here?" I asked, watching Forge and I disappear through the door. "I mean, if he's really that fast..."

He was flipping through camera angles quicker than I could track, his eyes missing nothing, as he stopped on one screen that showed the intersection halfway between the distillery and here.

"There's no sight of him there. Not so much as a blip." He fast-forwarded back to where Dobson appeared in the backyard. "He knew exactly when we'd be pulling up the driveway."

"Maybe it's just a coincidence. He could have guessed..."

"Selena," Forge said softly, pulling me closer to the screen, until I was pressed into him. "He was waiting for us, which means…"

I looked up at him, my stomach sinking. "I know what it means. There's someone at L&F who sold me out."

Sadly, that wasn't our only problem.

"There's something I have to tell you, Forge. In between the Scottish bloodbath and the plane ride home…I guess I forgot." How I'd forgotten something this momentous, I didn't know, but I'd been attacked, mentally assaulted and lied to, and somewhere in the middle of all of that, apparently, my brain had stopped working.

"The Elder wasn't just after you." I sighed, knowing exactly where this was going to lead. "He knew about me. He wasn't surprised to see me at Assembly—he *expected* me. Factor in the mysterious note that sent me to find you…and I have a feeling we've both been set up."

Even as his eyes began to glow, I warned him, "But don't, for one minute, think I'm staying locked up in here, Forge. I'm not a princess, and you don't have a tower high enough to keep me in."

The next few days were a stress-fest.

Forge didn't leave my side, while I looked at everyone at the company like they'd grow fangs and jump out of a dark corner, and didn't get a damn thing accomplished.

I didn't ask Forge what he'd done with Dobson's body, and he didn't feel the need to tell me.

He'd just returned from patrolling the perimeter, also known as the aging barns and the parking lot, on the lookout for a pack of rabid vampires heading to kidnap me. I tapped my pencil hard enough on my desk that it broke into pieces, one of them flying behind the filing cabinets.

Calm down, Selena. I made a circuit of the building and grounds, and there's no sign of vampires.

If there was, would you even tell me?

We were in our respective offices, ever since I'd kicked him out of mine, in order to put some distance between us. While I appreciated his protective fervor, he was driving me absolutely crazy.

We decided to tell the truth.

Yes, we did. But sometimes...people keep things from other people, just because it might upset them.

Not this time.

Promise?

What was the point of being in separate offices if all we did was think back and forth? I tossed the broken half-pencil in the wastebasket. Worse yet, being in Forge's head was starting to feel natural to me, and I didn't want it to be. I wanted it to continue being strange and foreign so I could maintain some distance between us.

I could stay out of your head. But you're thinking too loudly today, and I can't shut you out.

I lunged out of my chair and stalked to his office.

"We need to talk like normal people here," I told him sternly. "Or else everyone around here will think..."

"What will we think?" Emerson said from behind me. I jumped, because I'd thought Forge and I were the only ones down here.

"What's wrong?" I asked. Because the only time Emerson came to the basement was if something was wrong. I hadn't seen much of him lately, which hopefully meant the company was running smoothly. Not that I'd know, since I was more concerned with being kidnapped.

"Nothing. Just coming to give you a report that the barley is ready to go into the kiln for drying. Tomorrow morning, I have a crew ready to start turning it." He gave Forge a nod. "If you want to stick around late tonight, Selena can walk you through the process."

I winced as Forge's eyes settled on me. I hadn't exactly filled him in on my plans. Obviously, Emerson was way ahead of me.

All I'd wanted was a few hours of normalcy in the malting room, which didn't involve anything except me and the job that I loved. Sending Forge home early had been the first step in my plan, and now that was ruined.

"I'd love to show you how we do things here," I told him with false brightness, well aware he had eons more practice than I did at this stuff. "How does it smell?" I asked Emerson, my feet already moving.

"Perfectly rancid. Waiting for your special touch," he replied, grinning. He'd always hated the smell of malting, but loved the smell of mash. Go figure.

When were you going to tell me about this, Selena?

Not until I had to, Mr. Forge.

Forge silently fumed the whole way upstairs and over to the malting building, where we ducked in a side door and I took a deep breath. Sweet and sugary, like a rich honey. I didn't know why Emerson hated this smell so much—it was our lifeblood, and every time I smelled it, I knew another batch would be put into the oak barrels, and after twelve or more years, it could go anywhere in the world.

Look, I'm sorry. I just needed some time alone. Life has been... intense lately.

Slowly, his anger subsided, replaced by concern. *That's all you had to say, Miss Langston. I would have understood.* He reached out and plucked my sleeve. "I'm sorry, Selena. Your life has changed completely, and I know it's been hard."

"It has been," I said. "I'm tired of my emotions swinging between panic and fear. All of this"—I swung my hand around in the air—"relaxes me. It's simple, and uncomplicated, and familiar."

He nodded, then a mischievous smile curved his lips. *I don't care what Holloway says. This place smells heavenly.*

I fought the chuckle rising in me. *Heavenly? You are such a romantic,* I joked, skirting the piles of germinated green malt. When I'd reached the center of the floor, I crouched down and scooped up a handful. It was slightly moist and fragrant, and on the cusp of being ready.

But to be perfect, there was one more step, something that no distillery did anymore, because it was considered unnecessary and expensive and old-fashioned. The malt needed to be turned once more, and everyone else had gone home for the day.

I'm an old hand at turning malt. How long do we have?

Maybe six hours. I have a system, believe it or not, of telling when it's ready to go into the kiln.

Forge's laugh echoed through the metal building. "That's the middle of the night."

"Very good, Forge," I teased. "It's no wonder you've survived forever—you're wickedly observant."

He bumped me with his elbow, and I smiled back. "Can I help you?"

"And not afraid of manual labor, besides." I laughed. "There are coveralls on the hooks, and rakes there." I waved to the far wall. "If we start now, we might be done by midnight."

I don't have anywhere else I'd rather be.

Regretting my earlier crack about him being a romantic, I headed for the coveralls. I'd dressed in preparation for this, and slipped the coveralls over a t-shirt and formfitting yoga pants, but Forge had on a suit and tie.

He tossed his obviously expensive jacket onto one of the dusty hooks and undid his tie. By the time he was peeling off his shirt, I was walking to get us rakes. I did *not* need to see Forge shirtless right now. Not when I'd been spending far too much time imagining him in Scotland, circling Cade, his muscles flexing.

"Rake," he called, then deftly caught the one I threw. "Where do you want to start?"

"I don't think it matters," I answered, which was how we spent five hours, side by side, turning over malt in the barn. When we were done, and completely covered in dust, I grinned as I reached up and flicked a chunk of barley from his cheek. My fingers skimmed his skin, as smooth and cool as marble.

Before I could react, he snagged my wrist, stopping me in my tracks. For a second, we stayed frozen like that, his grip tightening as desire gleamed in his eyes.

"Forge..."

I didn't know what I was going to say. Maybe a joke to lighten the mood. Maybe a smart-ass retort about Mr. Fancy Pants raking barley.

Forge pulled me into him, and this time there was no awkwardness as we collided.

Our lips snagged on each other's, then Forge's hand went to my lower back and crushed me against him as he kissed me, his tongue slipping between my lips. Between the heady sweetness of the barley and my brain spinning at how good Forge tasted, I got lost in the moment.

Damn, but Forge could kiss, exploring my mouth with a thoroughness I truly admired. *Practice makes perfect.* When the thought popped into my head, I pulled away slightly. "Forge..." I said again, with as much luck as before, and he sucked my lower lip between his teeth. I felt the slight prick of fangs, and my knees almost gave out.

Fuck it. I'm tired of playing around.

I clasped his neck, pulling him back down to me. This time I was the aggressor, my tongue tangling with his as the kiss went on forever. I heard Forge's laughter in my head, and his other hand wrapped around my nape as he bent me backward.

I've been waiting for weeks for you to say those words.

I might have argued, but I couldn't focus on anything right now except Forge's tongue in my mouth, the feel of his corded, sweaty body pressed against me, the strength of his hands steadying me, and the fact that he'd just helped me rake barley.

It was stupid, but after working beside him tonight, Bastian Forge had changed in my eyes. No longer the legendary vampire, no longer a myth, but someone who enjoyed—and valued—the same things as I did.

Something between us solidified, something more than even this kiss, which was so delicious that I never wanted it to end.

We fell into the Range Rover, still dust-covered and sweaty, our hands going everywhere at once. After a couple of tries, I managed to start the vehicle, while Forge slid a hand under my coveralls and found my breast. I yanked him to my mouth, not caring about security cameras. Or anything else, for that matter.

For the first time in my life, I felt wanton, sexy...*desired*.

"We'll never get home if you keep that up," I said, pushing him away with a sigh. "You navigate and I'll drive."

Easier said than done. Forge didn't stop touching me until we finally arrived back at home and I threw the vehicle into park. "Home," I said, then our mouths crashed together once more. Something about kissing Forge had my thoughts all tangled up, and it was several more minutes before we stumbled from the car hand in hand and giggling.

I'm not giggling.

You are so. Like a little girl.

I dropped his hand and raced up the steps, only to have him intercept me before I reached the door, folding his arms around me.

How did you do that?

I moved from one place to another. Instantaneously.

He grinned, his fangs glinting in the moonlight. I was about to call him a show-off, but asked instead, "If you can dematerialize, then why am I driving you everywhere?"

"Because I find it more enjoyable to drive into work with you. It gives us more time together."

IF SELENA only knew what she looked like right now...

She'd forgotten to mask her emotions, and I watched them play across her face. Desire. Wonder. *Delight*, as my words registered with her. They were true. I'd driven into work with her because she was more talkative when she was driving. She told me things she wouldn't have otherwise, and I did the same. In fact, the drives were something I looked forward to, even though I could have been at the distillery in mere seconds.

I slid my fingers across her face, pushing a curl behind her ear.

Shower?

Hmm. We are very, very dirty.

My cock was hard already, but with her words, it pressed against the zipper almost painfully. I took the opportunity to tip her head back and take her mouth again, her lips opening wide to allow my tongue entrance. She tasted like honeyed peaches, and the more I tasted, the more I wanted. With effort, I broke away from her mouth, running my thumb over her lips.

"Selena, we can slow this down..." She stopped me by slapping her hand to my chest, where a cloud of white dust issued. "Or...we can continue on." I smiled down at her, taking in her lust-clouded eyes, pink cheeks, her puffy lips slightly apart. "I believe we were talking about getting cleaned up."

I ran my fingertips down her throat to the top of the ugly coveralls she was wearing, the shapeless gear completely obscuring her curves.

"But first, we really should get you undressed."

We left a trail of discarded clothes up the staircase, down the hallway to my room and into the bath. I had on my trousers and nothing else, and she was outfitted in a pair of panties and a thin bra. My hands roamed over her while hers explored my body, every featherlight touch making my cock jump. Fused to her lips, I turned on the water, hearing the pipes rattle slightly as the water made its way upstairs.

As the steam rose around us, I lifted Selena up and set her on top of me, then stripped off her bra. I lathered up my hands and scrubbed them up and down her back, the slippery friction raising goosebumps, her arms around my neck as she slowly explored my mouth, before pausing when she reached my fangs. I opened wider as she tentatively touched the tip of one with her tongue, then pushed against it, flooding my mouth with her blood.

I sucked her tongue into my mouth, drawing out her sweetness. I couldn't get enough. Even though I'd recently fed, I was ravenous for her, my synapses going wild as the taste of her hit my gut. She moaned and slid down into my lap, straddling my hips, and when her core settled onto my cock, she slid along the length of it, her eyes closed, head thrown back and shallow breaths coming fast.

I WAS SITTING in Forge's lap, surrounded by steam, our bodies sliding against each other as we vied for a good position. He was kissing me as if he were a dying man and I was water, and I was rubbing against his cock, trying to generate enough friction to get myself off. Normally, I'd be appalled at my actions, my total lack of control.

Sex had never felt like this—not this heady, reckless, wild feeling that made me want more and more until I was limp and satisfied. Apparently, Forge was a drug and I was addicted. And we hadn't actually even had sex yet. Part of me was panting for him to be inside me; the other part was thoroughly enjoying this slippery make-out session. Besides, the sooner we had sex, the sooner this would be over, and I didn't want it to end.

I dimly realized I still had my panties on, and they were the only thing standing between us.

Forge slid his finger beneath the band. "Lean back, Selena," he said, then wiggled them off, his hands sliding down my legs. Without my grip around his neck, I tilted back, then fell backward into the tub, water sloshing over the edge.

"Oh shit, I can't believe I just did that." I pushed my wet hair out of my face and found Forge grinning at me, his face completely unguarded. If I'd thought him handsome before, now he was breathtaking. I forgot all about the water on the floor and cupped his face in my hands, sliding back into his lap. As I rocked slightly against him, his fingers danced up and down my back, and we kissed again, slower this time, deeper as his hands slid down even further and cupped my ass.

Forge stood, taking me with him, and, spraying water all over everything, strode into his bedroom.

I'd missed it on entry, but now, looking over his shoulder

as he threw me on the bed, I took in the room, and the massive bed I'd landed on. "Holy crap. Why isn't my room like this?" Thick Turkish rugs carpeted the floor, while above me rose a huge four-poster bed, the tops of the posts carved to look like trees, their branches interwoven above us. I sank deeper into the velvet throw, the softness caressing my naked skin.

Forge crawled up and straddled me, his arms braced on either side of my head. "You can still back out, Selena. We can call it a night if this is too much."

I ran my hands down over his chest, the wide plane of his pecs, before my fingers bumped down along his ribbed abdomen. When I wrapped my hand around his cock, his face changed. It became harder, his eyes glittering in the darkness.

"No backing out. Not tonight," I told him, stroking him up and down, marveling at how soft the skin was, and how hard the steel underneath. With an almost inaudible groan, he pulled away, but still loomed over top me.

"Where should I start?" he teased, dipping his head to catch my nipple between his teeth while my body jerked. "These are nice," he said before switching to the other one, his tongue smoothing over the little nip of pain. "But I think I want to start a little bit lower." His mouth traced a path down to my belly button. When he moved even lower, I moved to cover myself up.

"I don't know if I can do that," I whispered, dropping my eyes. It wasn't that I hadn't imagined oral sex—it was more that I'd *only* imagined it, having never had anyone go down on me before.

"That's your call," he said, his tongue doing circles around my belly button. He lifted his eyes and met mine. "I'd be happy to oblige either way."

He wasn't pushing me, so why was I hesitating? With Forge, I felt safe. I trusted him and knew he'd take care of me. This odd reluctance made no sense.

"I *want* to taste you," Forge said, maybe seeing my doubt, cupping me between the legs, his thumb finding my clit and rubbing a slow, deliberate circle. A shudder rippled through me, my core tightening.

If this is what Forge can do with his thumb, just imagine what his tongue can do.

"Okay," I said, somewhat doubtful about the whole thing. I propped myself up on my elbows, watching his face as he planted a kiss on my stomach. As his tongue swirled around my belly button again, I discovered that I couldn't take my eyes from him.

I fully expected him to dive in, but instead he moved down my body and ran his hands up and down my calves, stroking me soothingly, going slightly higher each time, until my body was tensed up, and I silently urged him higher. I didn't know what kind of magic Forge was wielding tonight, but I welcomed it. I'd never felt this good before. Every time I reached a new high, he pushed me even higher.

He gently ran his hands up the insides of my thighs, planting kisses along the way. Pressing my legs apart, he slid his arms beneath my knees, then lifted them over his shoulders. I should have been horrified, but instead I was completely caught up in how I felt, and the look on Forge's face. He looked entranced as he leaned in and flicked my clit with his tongue.

My arms gave out and I fell back onto the bed, overtaken by the sensations rippling through me with every stroke of his tongue. As many times as I'd imagined this, Forge took it to a whole new level. I'd never thought I'd beg for release, but as Forge's name flew from my mouth, along with utter gibberish, everything I knew about sex went out the window.

"Selena?" he growled, moving back up my body, licking his lips. His face looked pained as he murmured hoarsely, "I don't think I can stop. Please…"

"Yes," I told him, arching my back and widening my hips for him.

He hung his head, then positioned himself, sliding the head of his shaft along my pussy, until he pushed in. Just a little, testing me. He was huge. Even though I'd held him in my hand a few minutes ago, he felt enormous. Inch by inch he pushed in, his eyes closed as he stretched me to bursting, blowing out a breath when he was fully seated.

"Are you okay?" he asked softly. I nodded, my hands on his shoulders, feeling the bunching of his muscles as he slowly pulled out. With a groan, he pushed back in, until he was embedded to the hilt.

Every nerve in my body was tingling, every part of me focused on how he tightly fit inside me, the heat as he slid in and out, the escalating response of my body to his, while we moved in tandem. I was close, so close, but my orgasm kept flitting out of reach.

Then he pushed me down into the bed and hooked my leg under his arm before slamming into me. The angle was perfect, and he drove in deeper than before. I squeezed my eyes shut, determined to feel nothing except Forge inside me. My muscles locked up, then quivered as my climax broke free, the sensation roaring through me, my core tightening up, my back arching off the bed, my fingernails digging into Forge's shoulders.

He laughed in my ear, low and sensual, before pulling out and slamming home a final time, his guttural groan as he came making my toes curl up.

Weeks, Selena, he murmured in my head as he collapsed beside me and gathered me up. *I've been waiting weeks for this.*

SELENA WAS sound asleep when I left her in bed, tugging on a pair of sweats.

I materialized in the library, rounding the desk as the monitor came to life. I'd been too distracted on the drive home to be a hundred percent focused on our surroundings, and wanted to confirm we didn't have any undead intruders tonight.

A quick scan of the video footage told me we'd made it through another night untouched, then I navigated over to the program I'd had running in the background for days. Human financial institutions were easy enough to hack into these days, especially since the Society had come up with a program to research potential prospects. Pages of financial records cascaded on the screen, but there was only one I was interested in.

As I saw the name on the top of the screen, I blew out a deep breath.

An offshore account, with lots of recent activity, mostly withdrawals.

Selena had done a good job of shielding herself from hurt. Fuck knows there'd been enough of it in her life.

But this was going to break her damn heart, and I only had a couple of hours to decide how I was going to tell her.

26

As I coasted down the dark driveway in neutral, I congratulated myself on sneaking out of the house without Forge noticing. A small but significant accomplishment, when your opponent seemingly knew everything.

"Not this morning, Forge. This morning, I'm going to surprise *you* for once."

There was a bakery less than a mile away, and thoughts of fresh cinnamon rolls and coffee danced in my head as I made the turn onto the main road, starting the engine as I did.

Since I'd woken up all alone, I was salty enough to not leave a note, figuring if he'd wanted to see me this morning, he should have stayed in bed.

Last night had been...

Well, last night had been the best ever, but with Forge, I'd learned not to get too comfortable, since life with him always seemed prone to change. But damn, that man could kiss. As well as several other skills I'd like to repeat. Just to make sure last night wasn't a fluke.

Truthfully, I didn't know what to make of the two of us. In a matter of weeks, Forge had wormed his way into my bed. Into my heart, damn it.

It was so early that no one was on the roads, and when I pulled into the bakery, the streetlights were just turning off. Forge and I had stopped here before for coffee on our way into work, and I was dying for a huge cinnamon roll dripping in frosting.

It occurred to me that if Forge and I spent our nights tangled up in each other, I'd probably burn off enough calories to have sweets whenever I wanted. A total win, in my opinion.

I dropped the keys into my pocket and pulled on the door. Locked.

"Well, it is early," I told myself, turning to get back in the car, but then my feet stopped moving completely, and the keys fell from my hand. What I was seeing couldn't be real. I blinked to make sure, and still saw the same thing. It just couldn't be.

Brandon—*my dead brother*—was leaning back on the hood of the Rover, arms crossed over his chest, a gloating expression on his face.

"Ah, there she is, the good Langston. Been a while, Selena."

That conceited, self-congratulatory look was the last thing I saw as I was grabbed from behind and a hood was thrown over my head.

27

Brandon was an asshole, but he was a chatty asshole. He and I had never developed the usual brother-sister bond that siblings have, mostly because he was either in jail, or on the run during my formative years. The few times I'd seen him, he'd come looking for Dad to bail him out, or, when that failed, breaking into the safe at work and taking whatever he needed.

Right now, he was detailing his latest scam. Namely, kidnapping me for the Elder.

"...then all I had to do was disappear for a few years. Piece of cake."

One more thing: my brother had been born without a conscience. Its absence was especially apparent to me as he described how much money he'd be making off me, without a care of what would happen to me in the process.

People who said blood was thicker than water had never met Brandon Langston.

Since my hands were bound behind me and I had a hood over my head, I had no choice but to listen to his verbal diarrhea, although I made it a point to kick out every so often, happy when I finally heard him grunt in pain.

"You always were a little bitch," my brother snarled. "Which was why it was so easy to put the company up as collateral. I almost wish I'd stuck around to watch you scramble to save that worthless relic."

"What happened to Dad?" I asked, sick to my stomach at what I was about to hear. But I had to know. I *had* to know what Brandon had done.

"Dad? Dad did what he always did: he came to talk some sense into me. I told him I didn't need his bullshit motivational speeches. I needed cash. He didn't get it." Brandon went silent for a minute. "*He never got it.*"

"How did he die? *Who was in that car with him?*" My nerves were at the boiling point, but I swore I'd at least hear the truth before I died. Because there was no doubt that was where I was headed.

"He went quick, if that's any consolation. The other body?" Brandon took a noisy slurp, the sound at total odds with our morbid discussion, not that Brandon would recognize that, the heartless bastard. "Just some druggie off the street. The Elder has a way... It's fantastic. He pulled all the blood out, then put some of mine into the corpse. It worked —they ID'd the body as me, and of course Dad was in the car, which sealed the deal."

My stomach was churning. *Poor Dad.*

"When did the Elder get involved?" I studiously kept myself from imagining Dad's final moments, the disappointment he must have felt. How afraid he must have been. I'd hated my brother for years, but that hate was a pale imitation of what I felt for him now.

"Don't know how he found me, but he did," Brandon said, then took another loud drink. "He proposed a deal. I sink the company into enough debt to send you to that vampire who helped start the distillery." Beside me, I felt the bastard shrug. "It was easy enough. A few weeks of steady gambling, and a loan shark who'd accept the company as collateral. Bada-bing, bada- boom, the company is sinking fast, and you'll do anything to save it."

His face got really close to mine. "Face it, Selena, you're predictable as hell."

Without thinking, I head-butted him, the crack as our skulls connected echoing through my head. "I hope you're bleeding. I hope that hurt like a fucking bitch," I snarled through the hood. "But most of all, I hope you get what's undoubtedly coming to you."

"If you mean the millions I'll collect when I deliver you, then yes, I'll get what I deserve."

His words were muffled enough that I thought I might have broken his nose.

"One thing's for sure, I don't know what the Elder wants you for, but I'd sure rather be me than you right now."

The rest of the interminable ride was spent in silence, thank God, since I thought I might throw myself from the car if my brother kept running his mouth. When the vehicle slowed, and gravel crunched beneath the tires, Brandon muttered, "Finally."

From a safe distance.

I'd put my shield up the second the hood went over my head. It was safe to assume our driver wasn't human, and now that we'd arrived, vampires would be waiting. Maybe even the Elder.

"I'd say good luck, but where you're going, you'll need more than that." Brandon's voice was venomous as the door opened and I was bathed in cold air. "See you around, sis. Or not."

28

I 'd been gone for less than an hour.

As I quickly scrolled through the camera footage, I kept reminding myself of that.

She couldn't have gone far.

Except I reached out through our bond and didn't feel a thing.

I switched to the line of cameras I'd installed on the main road, as a precaution should anyone decide to do something this stupid. I watched the Rover roll silently down the driveway, then the headlights come on as she turned over the engine. The angle was enough that I also saw Selena's face light up in satisfaction as she drove toward the distillery. Probably thrilled she escaped unnoticed.

Within seconds, I materialized in the basement. Her office was empty, the lights off.

No sign of Holloway, either.

I flew from one location to the other—the aging barns, the malting building, back to the main building—before I started losing my shit. There was no sign of her at work, but there was a bakery we'd stopped at, and I remembered how she'd swooned over the donuts.

I materialized in the parking lot, my heart loosening as I saw the Range Rover parked out front. A steady stream of customers went in and out, and I stepped inside, scanning the small interior. No sign of her, not so much as a hair. Thoroughly frustrated, I stepped up to the counter.

"Where is the woman who drives *that*?" I impatiently hitched my thumb at the Rover.

The girl's face brightened. "Oh, good, you finally came to get the truck. It's been there since I opened." She bent over and began digging beneath the register. "Here you go."

The keys to the Rover landed on the glass-covered menu, and I stared at them blankly for a second before my brain caught up. "Why do you have the keys?"

"Like I said, they were on the ground when I got here, lying right in front of the truck. Thanks for coming to get them." She tilted her head, then asked, "Would you like to place an order?"

I whirled away and drove toward home.

Someone had taken Selena. And I knew exactly who.

WHEN THEY YANKED the hood off, my brother was nowhere in sight.

The Elder was even uglier in the bright light of day, his skin so thin that I could see the blue veining beneath, even from here. His ubiquitous bodyguards loomed behind him like twin bookends, and there was nothing but farmland as far as I could see. Somewhere close to route seventy-six, since we'd been driving fast, until we'd gotten off the highway moments ago.

Somewhere Forge would never find me, I thought, my heart sinking.

I'd evidently hurt myself as badly as I'd hurt Brandon, because I felt the knot growing on my forehead, even as the Elder's gaze strayed to it and he frowned. "Who injured the human? I gave strict orders—not a hair on her head was to be harmed."

Well, that was good to know. At least he wasn't planning on killing me outright.

"She did it to herself," Brandon insisted as he oozed up to join us. "She's always been a mean, stubborn little bitch." I noted the look of distaste on the guards' faces. As well as the Elder's. *Someone doesn't like you very much, Brandon.*

"So you say," the Elder commented drily, motioning a guard closer. The huge vampire bent down as the Elder whispered something, then stepped back at attention. "Nevertheless, she will remain untouched."

"Well, I was right, wasn't I?" Brandon called out as the Elder did the weird gliding thing straight toward me. "I told you she'd do anything to save that company, and she did."

The old vampire drew closer as Brandon watched on in fascination. Hands held me in position as he closed in, every inch of me shrinking away. Up close...well, I just wish I didn't have to see what he looked like up close and personal. He was horrendous—I could see rot growing just below the surface of his face, the blue veins seemed to actually wiggle and his eyes were milky in the sunlight, one of them almost white.

"You eluded Dobson," he said. "Where is he now?"

Not about to give this asshole anything, I clamped my mouth shut. Predictably, the squirmy sensation creeped through my skull as I put every ounce of effort into propping up my shields. After a minute, he gave up, leaving me nauseated and sweaty.

"He's dead," the Elder said, satisfaction in his voice. "I don't need to read your thoughts to know."

We engaged in a short, pointless staring contest until I decided I didn't want to look into his gross eyes anymore.

"You will be taken back to Scotland, where you will perform the same task you did for Forge. Except"—his gaze turned keen—"this time, there will a high cost for failure, as well as for any small betrayals. You may believe yourself free, but that would be a mistake. You answer to me from now on, and me alone. Consider me your...*keeper*." A flash of pointed yellow teeth was the closest he got to humor.

"Why me?" I asked, genuinely curious. "How did you know to target me?"

"You are the first female born in the Langston family in centuries. Ambrose Langston had a touch of Fae, but as a female..." His veined hands clenched at his sides. "It was logical you'd possess the full ability, as it's passed to descendants through the blood, and only to females."

Well, at least I finally had an explanation for my gift. Such that it was.

"Did Forge happen to mention to you how he and your ancestor met?"

When I didn't deign to answer, he went on, a hint of his strange accent creeping into the words.

"He killed one of us, to protect that human." The Elder's face tightened. "My predecessor, if it can be believed. A human killing an Elder. The clan could not believe it happened, and for that alone, we should have hunted him down and killed him. But instead...Mara became fascinated with the human. Once she'd turned him, he became one of us, and was expected to forget about his human life. And his human friends." The Elder said the word *friend* as if it were poison on his tongue. Suddenly, I understood just how lonely Bastian had been all these years, surrounded by nothing but poisonous snakes.

Strangely enough, Mara's name didn't bring on the surge of jealousy it had before, as if somehow I'd made my peace with her and Forge's past.

"What do you want from me?" I asked.

"You are going to make me the most powerful vampire in the world, not just of the Highland clans. You've only touched the surface of your ability—once you are properly motivated, I intend to use you as a weapon against my enemies."

"Huh. Good luck with that." I snorted, twisting my hands against the restraints. "I'll never do anything for you, much less help you take over the world." Seriously, why couldn't people just be happy with what they had? Besides, this guy was a physical wreck—good luck ruling the world while you fell apart.

He went on as if I hadn't spoken. "You will uncover any plots against me, ferret out my opponents' weaknesses and determine whom I can trust. If you are correct in your predictions, you will continue to live. If you fail me..."

"Once again, I'll never do anything for you, least of all help you get more power."

"Brave words, human. Brave words."

There was a scrambling sound, and one of the bookend bodyguards dragged Emerson Holloway in front of me, his hands bound, just like mine, his hair askew, his glasses gone. If there was one thing Emerson hated, it was when he lost his glasses.

"Are you all right?" he asked.

I nodded, looking him over for any apparent injuries.

Aside from his rumpled appearance, he seemed unharmed. But I had to admit, the Elder certainly knew how to choose the right leverage, as the bodyguard's fangs extended and he bent Emerson sideways to expose his throat.

I only lasted a second before I stopped this madness.

"Fine," I spat. "I'll do what you want. Just don't hurt him."

Gratitude shone in Emerson's eyes as the bodyguard relaxed his grip and set him back on his feet effortlessly, as if he were a child. "I'm sorry, Selena," Emerson said quietly, as if he had anything to apologize for. "I tried, but I couldn't outrun them."

If we weren't facing down death, I would have laughed at the mental picture of Holloway trying to outrun vampires, but as it was, there was nothing funny about this. I was going to have to comply with this asshole Elder's demands, at least until Forge found me, which was the hope I was hanging on to right now.

"Set him free, and I'll go with you," I said, keeping my eye on Emerson, who was looking paler by the minute. "It's not like you don't know where he's going to be. If you're going to use him as leverage, he's no good to you dead."

Not the best argument, but all I wanted right now was to keep my old friend alive. Maybe he could tell Forge what happened. What my asshole brother had done, yet again.

"Very well," the Elder agreed. "Wipe his mind. I don't want to leave a trail for Forge."

I watched helplessly as the bodyguard did some voodoo bullshit and Emerson's face smoothed out, his eyes going blank. *So much for that plan.*

29

I 'd spent hours going over the footage frame by frame, looking for any small clue that would help me track Selena. While I knew who'd taken her, I didn't know where, though my plane was already waiting on the tarmac, with a flight plan filed for Scotland.

Cursing my limited abilities—if only I could materialize directly to Scotland—I shut down the computer, grabbed a coat and re-emerged at the airport. With luck, the pilot could cut an hour off the travel time, but the Elder would have a head start.

As I boarded the plane, I reached out once more to Selena: *Stay calm, remember your training and, for the love of God, don't do anything stupid.*

I was smiling when I boarded, only because if she *had* heard me, she'd be fuming over that last bit.

FINALLY, after my usual take-off panic attack, they'd untied my hands, though it took hours before I could hold a glass of water without dropping it. For some unfathomable reason, Brandon was accompanying us, but I had the feeling that it wasn't for the reasons he thought. I figured the Elder viewed him more like a loose end than a valuable member of the team. But I couldn't waste my time on Brandon, not when there were so many other things to worry about.

Like whether or not Emerson still had his faculties.

If Forge had figured out where I was.

How I'd get out of this mess.

All these problems intertwined in my head until I thought I'd go mad. The only bright side was that the Elder, and his henchmen, left me alone. I guessed there wasn't anywhere for me to go at forty thousand feet. For the time being, I was stuck obsessing.

I spent some time poking around in the bodyguard's heads, but as expected, they knew nothing. They operated under a do-as-I'm-told directive, and other than a few worthless tidbits—one of them was very, very hungry—I got nothing. As for the Elder, we went back and forth the entire flight, studiously ignoring each other, while trying to break through each other's shields.

Good news: he wasn't successful.

Bad news: neither was I.

We landed in Scotland in the middle of the night, and as we disembarked the Elder's plane—a rattling, antiquated dinosaur compared to Forge's—I wanted to kiss the ground.

I didn't know where we were—some outpost of human civilization, from the looks of it—but at least I was back on terra firma, and alive.

"*Scotland.*" Brandon sidled up beside me as if we were now besties. "Can you believe it, Selena? I never thought I'd get here, even though Dad told us a thousand times he'd take us." He'd been drinking steadily on the plane, and from his numerous disappearances to the bathroom, I assumed he'd been snorting, injecting or smoking as well.

I walked in silence toward the waiting car, the body-guards an ominous wall behind me, herding me onward. Brandon didn't shut up, and I prayed he wouldn't be riding with me to wherever we were going.

Unfortunately, that was one prayer God didn't answer.

SELENA WAS in the wind by the time my plane landed in Edinburgh, but it was a small matter to get myself to the outskirts of Falkirk. The Elder wasn't here, but someone else was.

"Awrite—you in there?" I called, while I rapped on the derelict cottage's door. Little more than a potting shed, there was a tendril of peat smoke coming from the chimney, so I knew the bastard was here.

"Fuck off."

At least he'd answered in English, so he knew it was me.

"Open the door, Cade. I need your help."

I heard him coming, heavy, resentful footsteps before the door was thrown open and he filled up the opening. "I must not have heard you right. It sounded like you need my help."

True, I'd arranged our blood match, knowing the Elder would choose Cade as his champion.

Also true: if he helped me, I'd sworn to never involve him in my bullshit again. Too bad I was here less than a week later, breaking that promise.

"Damn it, Cade, let me in."

He leaned against the doorjamb, blocking my way. "Not too good at keeping promises, are you, mate?"

"The bastard took Selena. All I need is a location." I knew the Elder holed up somewhere between Callander and Strathyre. But right now, I didn't have time to search every bloody loch and valley in the Highlands.

Cade narrowed his eyes, deciding, I supposed, if that was a good enough reason to help me.

"You're going after the Elder by yourself?"

"I can handle him." Of that I was sure. Depending how many were with him...that might be another matter. "Just tell me where he is, and I'll leave you be."

Cade disappeared, then came back, slipping his coat on in the process. "Never hurts to have a bit of help," he said coolly, locking the door behind him as if anyone would be interested in breaking in. "Ever heard of Castle Runacraig?" When I shook my head, he grinned. "Follow along, then, laddie, and learn from the best."

His words hung on the air as we materialized, reappearing in a forest. Through the trees there were spotlights shining, and the faint scent of fire in the air.

We crept through the underbrush until the castle came into view. It jutted from the granite as if it were part of the mountain, one lone, scraggly tree on the east side, and a sheer drop-off on the north and west. The only approach was to the south, where a row of cars were parked haphazardly. A few guards milled around, one sitting on the car hood, smoking.

"They'll let me pass," Cade assured me softly. "Once I'm inside, I'll see if your human is still alive."

I hesitated. Cade and I were not friends. Instead, we used each other when we had to, in order to survive. I didn't exactly trust the sullen bastard, but he'd never crossed me before. I hoped he wouldn't this time.

"How will you get word to me?"

"You'll know," he said with a churlish snort, right before he vanished. I watched him reappear in front of the smoking guard, who dropped his cigarette. A few words between them and then Cade disappeared through the front gates. Then I waited. And waited.

A flash of fire exploded from a window, and I heard the crack of the blast a second later, strong enough that I felt it in my chest. The glow gilded the forest in yellow light.

Forge. Selena's voice echoed in my head. *I'm here.*

Reaching her was my only thought, and without hesitation, I materialized.

30

W hen we arrived, the Elder didn't waste any time.

The hood over my head, I was led to a room where a man, a vampire, was chained to a metal chair bolted to the stone floor. I averted my eyes the second I saw him. He was naked, and had been tortured, in awful ways that I couldn't—and didn't—want to imagine.

One of the bodyguards grabbed his hair and pulled his head up so he was looking at me, while the other one maneuvered me roughly into place in front of him. The chained vampire had been beaten so badly that both eyes were swollen shut, and dried blood matted his hair.

Brandon leaned against the wall, bracing his unsteady legs, but his eyes were bright as he surveyed the scene.

"Can I trust him?" the Elder asked, gliding into the room, showing his yellow teeth in an eager grimace that probably passed for a smile around here. "Or did he betray me?"

"I..." My mouth snapped shut as I realized this was my test. Maybe my only one. If I failed, not only would I be dead, but Holloway as well. If I was successful, this guy would die. "Fine," I said, thinking of ways I could keep all of us alive. "I'll do it. But it takes some time for me to get a feel for his thoughts—especially if there's been...damage."

Actually, the poor guy was easy to read. Pain, pain and more pain. I pushed past the waves of agony to what was left of his addled brain. *I didn't mean to... I tried...* He hadn't betrayed anyone, but he'd failed the Elder, and I supposed, in his book, that counted as deception.

"He's in too much pain for me to read him," I said flatly. "Next time, I suggest you leave me something to work with." I was sick as I said it, but passing the buck to someone else was the only way around this impossible situation.

"Kill him," the Elder ordered his bodyguards dispassion-ately. "Unless you'd like to change your story?"

I shook my head. If I told them what I'd seen, then they'd kill him anyway.

The guard's hand was poised at the vampire's throat, ready to rip it out, I supposed, when the entire room rocked back and forth, a cloud of gravel and dust showering us. I went down, as did Brandon and one of the guards.

Forge, I thought as loudly as I could. *I'm here.*

"Get outside and see what's happening," the Elder snarled, turning on his heel. "Lock the door behind us." He disappeared through the door, locking me, Brandon and the half-conscious vampire in together. With no windows in this room, I prayed the power held out.

Forge, I half screamed in my head. *Where are you?*

Right here, Selena. I'm coming. Hold on.

For the first time in hours, relief flooded through me. He was close enough to hear me, and just that little bit of knowledge caused tears to flood my eyes. I sniffed, and Brandon looked at me suspiciously.

"Dust," I told him, wiping the tears with my sleeve. "It gets to me every time."

"Why did they lock me in here with *you*?" Brandon whined. "I should be *outside*."

Surprise, big brother, you are nothing but a loose end. I hooked my fingers around the door handle and yanked, but it wouldn't budge. The smell of acrid smoke seeped beneath the door, along with a puff of black. Looking around, I was comforted by the fact everything was stone, so maybe we wouldn't burn to death.

The light overhead flickered slightly, smoke now swirling around it. The table in the corner was heaped with junk, but the shiny silver keys looked like they might belong to the shiny chains holding the vampire to the chair. I found a tattered blanket and laid it on the floor next to him, then fumbled with the keys and the locks until I worked his hands and ankles free.

"Help me with him," I told Brandon, my hands on the vampire's shoulders.

"Do it yourself," my brother retorted, pacing the length of the small room. "*I have to get out of here.*" He was getting jittery, which meant the drugs were wearing off. Pretty soon he'd realize he wasn't as useful as he thought, and then he'd panic. I so didn't want to be around for that.

I half dumped the poor guy onto the blanket, but at least he was free. Kneeling down beside him, I whispered softly, "If you can, you need to materialize out of here. I won't be able to get you out of here. I'm sorry."

Brandon's incessant pacing stopped. "Since when do you care about some piece-of-shit vampire more than you care about your own family?"

"I don't have a family anymore. You made sure of that."

"Oh, now you're going to have a pity party over Dad? He'd had a stroke—his days were numbered anyway."

All I could do was stare. When had he become so evil, or had he been born that way? "Shut up, Brandon, before I do something stupid." I drew a steadying breath. "You stole Dad's life, and in turn, mine as well. Because you are a selfish little bastard." I lifted my eyes to his. "And when the Elder finally kills you, I hope I'm there to see it."

THE SECOND I REAPPEARED, I heard Selena again. *Forge. Where are you?*

I landed right in the middle of the chaos, thick smoke rolling down the stairs and a clearly panicked guard hitting me in the chest, driving me into the stone wall. There was no sign of Cade, and the guard and I grappled for a moment before I threw him off me and headed for the steps. The explosion had come from the third level, so that was where I'd find Cade.

I fought my way upward through the smoke, leaving bodies in my wake, looking for any sign of Selena.

"Who the fuck are you?" I'd barely crested the top step when both of the posted guards converged on me. A knife sank deeply into my side as fangs tore at my other shoulder, instantly drenching me with blood. I feinted right, plowing through the cartilage in the guard's chest until my hand closed around his heart. I dropped it to the floor as I faced the other guard, but Cade got there first, snapping his neck with an audible pop.

"Better late than never," he said, his cool eyes raking me over. "No sign of your human, though."

Where are you? I shouted through the bond.

In a locked room. In the basement, maybe. I couldn't see.

"Basement?" I shouted to Cade. "Where is it?"

"Three levels down." He gestured toward the stairs. "You'll have to walk—everything is reinforced with steel, so there's no materializing. Locks are all copper."

I killed everything in my way as I took the steps three at a time, so focused on Selena that I didn't even take the time to make sure my enemies were dead, only to keep moving toward her.

31

I was trying the door again when it opened, throwing me halfway across the room.

Brandon was still whining about how he'd been shortchanged, and the beaten vampire was groaning in pain when the Elder and his henchmen flew through the door then slammed it shut behind them. Not quickly enough. I glimpsed the utter chaos outside, vampires rushing through the hall, smoke billowing along the ceiling.

Brandon stepped toward them, on the verge of asking a question when the Elder snapped. Faster than I could see, before I could even scream a warning, he was at Brandon's throat. The wet, ripping sound made me squeeze my hands over my ears, and then he dropped my brother's body to the floor before he advanced on me, his eyes glowing, his words low.

"Now. Tell me where that bastard is."

After that, everything happened so quickly.

Bastian materialized out of nothingness, surrounded by so many shadows that he looked like a winged avenger. He took one long look at me and vanished, reappearing behind one guard, then the next, disappearing before their bodies hit the floor.

The next thing I knew, I was behind him, blocked from the blood, the bodies on the floor and the Elder, who showed his displeasure with a long hiss.

"Impossible," the Elder screamed, his face going blue. "You can't materialize in here."

"Old dog, new tricks," Bastian said mildly, his hand finding mine and giving it a reassuring squeeze before it dropped to his side, his fingers curling in readiness. "You'd know that if you cared to keep up with the times."

The same sort of shadows that swirled around Bastian surrounded the Elder, almost masking his gloating smile. "I should have killed you all those years ago."

Bastian said nothing in response, but something shuddered through him—surprise, maybe—before he pushed me backward as the Elder's shadows shot forward and closed around him. My back struck the wall, harder than he'd probably intended, driving the breath out of me as I doubled over. When I was able to rise, Bastian was stockstill, bound—like he had bound Dobson—and unable to move.

"But now is as good a time as any," the Elder said, gliding forward, his fangs descending. The shadows were so dense that I could hardly even see Bastian now, his face disappearing from view as I watched in desperation.

I scrambled to reach Bastian, but the darkness kept me at bay, as if there were an invisible wall between us. He let out a low moan, and I clawed at it until my fingertips bled, but there was no getting through it.

Run, Selena. Run and find Cade. He'll get you out of here.

"No," I said, my hands scrambling against the Elder's magic. "I'm not leaving."

Please. You won't get another chance.

I couldn't break through the magic, but I might be able to break through the bastard's mind. I just had to want it badly enough. I hit his shield like a ram, the thing reverberating from my blow, and the old vampire stumbled back a step, then another as I continued my assault, not giving him an opportunity to shore up his defenses.

The second I found a crack, I pried it open and stabbed my consciousness through it, my only intention to hurt him as badly as he was hurting Bastian. A trickle of black blood ran from his nostril, more blooming in one clouded eye.

Encouraged, I pressed harder, deeper, driving into his consciousness with a brutality I hadn't thought I possessed. Within the shadows, Bastian groaned, and I felt a flicker of him in my head, helping shore up my own defenses, protecting me, just like he always did.

The Elder was breathing hard now, his shadows slipping enough that I saw Forge's face, bruised and bloodied, and pushed again. Something snapped within the Elder, some invisible barrier, and he went to his knees, blood spurting from seemingly everywhere as Forge reappeared.

One step and his hands were around the old vampire's head—a sharp twist, and his neck snapped every bit as easily as Brandon's. I sank to the floor, hands to my aching head as Bastian gathered me up. *Selena. I thought...*

"Are you all right?" he asked, his voice beyond gentle, but a hint of anger still vibrated beneath his calm words. Anger that wasn't directed at me, but at what had happened. Almost happened.

I could have lied. I usually did lie. "No," I said. "I'm not." Admitting it broke something inside me, and I sobbed, clutching Bastian's shirt.

Bastian slid his arms around me, holding me tight. For a

long time, we sat there together, my eyes tightly closed, my face buried in Bastian's chest as I tried to block everything out.

"I never wanted to believe he was this evil," I finally said, knowing he knew exactly who I was talking about. "If the Elder hadn't killed him"—I swallowed, the words like bile in my mouth—"I think I might have. I know I wanted to."

"If I could take this all away," Bastian murmured into my hair, "if I could do that for you, I would. I hate seeing you like this, and knowing there's nothing I can do to change it."

I sank deeper into his arms. "You already have."

The door crashed open, startling the half-dead vampire, who curled into a ball.

"Oi," Cade shouted. "There's guards to be killed, and I'm the only one doing the work while you're sitting in here on your arse."

"How...are you alive?" My voice faltered as I remembered Bastian ordering me to find Cade. "Are you *helping* us?"

"If doing all the work is helping, then yes."

"But I thought you were dead?"

Cade snorted. "It'll take more than this lightweight to kill me."

"He threw the fight, of course," Forge said with a wink, as Cade glowered at the both of us. "You don't actually think I could beat him in a fair fight?"

Cade shrugged, his shoulders bunching. "We had our share of go-arounds when we were pups, but Forge's right—he fights too clean for me. No eye-gouging for the high and mighty Forge." Cade pursed his lips as he looked at us. "Of course, now that the Elder's dead, it leaves this fine establishment up for grabs."

Bastian shook his head, holding me tighter. "I don't want any part of this. How about you?"

"I could get used to this. Been living rough for too long now." Cade surveyed our surroundings with a sour look on his face. "Redecorating will be in order."

"I'd say so," Bastian said, a touch of his humor returning. "But don't look at me. You're on your own." He paused. "My only request—"

"Ah, now we're making requests."

"—would be to have my privileges restored." He gave me a hard squeeze. "I'd like to have my distillery back, and my land."

"It's all yours," Cade said with a wave of his hand. "So long as you help me whip these bastards into shape and back me for Elder."

32

W e left Cade in charge of the clusterfuck at the castle, as Selena had started calling it, and headed for my plane. We'd be in Philadelphia by sunrise. As keen as I was to set down roots in Scotland again, I didn't think she'd be half as eager, not after tonight.

"We're going home," I said firmly, surveying her frozen face, the lingering shock and fear. "Then you can decide what comes next."

"I have no idea," she whispered, her voice hoarse. "I don't even know...where to start with all of this."

She'd been quiet the entire ride, but she hadn't let go of me either, her hands wrapped around my arm like vises, her face pale. Her brother... If I agreed with Selena about anything, it was his death. Not that death would erase everything he'd done to her. Taken from her.

"In time," I said carefully, unsure how she'd take this, when the pain was so fresh, "you will come to terms with what he did. Not forgive him, but learn to deal with it, so it does not hurt so badly."

"I don't know...maybe," she whispered. "I was so

surprised to see him, leaning against the Rover, looking exactly like the last time I saw him. I thought... For a split second, I thought he was a ghost. Then I knew."

Brandon Langston had been the one I was tracking the morning I'd left her alone, but I didn't think mentioning that right now would soothe any of her wounds.

"For years I tried to make him into a victim, I suppose. To cut him slack for his shortcomings, excuse his behavior. But the things he said about Dad...about me...there was something wrong with him, Bastian, something terribly wrong. And he didn't even know it."

We stopped in front of the plane, and I reached over and smoothed her hair back, then tipped her face up so she was looking in my eyes. "You can't fix other people, Selena. You couldn't have stopped him even if you'd tried."

"I know. But...now I know how Dad felt, all those times he tried. Hopeless."

I ushered her into the plane, Selena moving as if she was in a trance, never letting go of me. Not even when we were safely inside. She was a mess, we both were, but I was more concerned about what was going on in her head than her appearance at the moment.

Selena. Look at me.

There was an empty bleakness in her eyes, a hopeless-ness that was so at odds with her usual fire that I smoothed her hair back again. Just so I could keep touching her.

Oh, Bastian. She leaned further into me, and I folded her against my chest, my arms crossed over her back. Her fear was a sour tang in the air, but her trembling had stopped. Mostly.

I can't stop thinking about it. All the blood, my brother...the vampire. She pulled away from me. *Did you get him out? I told him we'd...*

Cade is taking care of it right now. He'll get him home safely.

Good. She closed her eyes and sank against me. *Good.*

I did something I'd never done before, and I hoped to never do again. I settled us into the nearest seat and touched her forehead lightly with my lips. *Sleep,* I told her silently. *Sleep, and it will go away for a while.*

ONCE AGAIN, I woke up on a plane in Bastian's arms. When he'd become Bastian to me and not Forge, I couldn't tell, but he was different now. *We* were different.

The last thing I remembered was falling asleep, my slumber so deep that even the bloodstained images of Scotland didn't penetrate the fog. I lifted my head, and my cheek peeled away from his shirt. "Ugh," I murmured. "We need to get cleaned up."

"We do," he agreed, not loosening his arms. "But you needed rest more than you needed a shower."

"Maybe so. But..." I lifted my hand, dirty and caked with dried blood where my nails had torn off. "Oh my, that looks...*bad*." Now that I was awake, I was aware of how my body ached. My very bones seemed to hurt.

"I didn't mean to push you so hard," Bastian said sheepishly. "I only thought of getting you away from the Elder's magic before he captured us both."

"I know," I said, still looking at my battered hands. "I suppose I can forgive you." A bleak attempt at humor, but it was a start, and some of the worry cleared from Bastian's eyes.

"Shower," he insisted. "Right now. I can't take another minute of seeing you covered in dirt and blood."

"You can't stand it?" I replied, my face too tight to smile.

"No, I can't. Into the shower. I have a clean shirt you can wear. I didn't think to bring—"

"Hush," I told him. "One of your shirts will be...lovely."

He settled me into the shower, and I had half a mind to ask him to join me, but we never would have fit. There was a moment of panic when he shut the door, then I stepped under the steaming spray. Reddish-brown water swirled down the drain, and I stood there until it was clear, scrubbing my hair, then running the suds over my body until I was reasonably clean.

His shirt was soft, expensive and hung well below my knees. I had to roll the sleeves up, but a minute later I stepped out of the shower, toweling my hair. "Your turn."

Forge wasn't in there nearly as long as I was, and I teased him about being a tree-hugging water conservationist when he emerged wrapped in nothing but a towel, steam misting the air.

Do you know what I need?

Clothes? I teased again. I *did* feel better, after sleep and a shower. Fragile still, but not quite so...breakable. Forge didn't have a mark on him, except for a slightly pink line on his side. The same side that had been drenched in blood earlier.

What is that? A bit of shock colored my words.

Knife wound. It's almost gone.

I shook my head at the utter craziness of that statement. *Is this my new life?* I wondered, knowing he could hear me. Wanting him to hear me. *Will it always be like this?*

No. His flat denial bolstered me up. *Our lives...* He corrected himself, Your *life will be whatever you want it to be. You just have to decide what you want.*

He watched me carefully from the other side of the cabin, making no move to come closer. Giving me time, and space, to decide what I wanted for myself. But I already knew. I'd wanted Bastian Forge since the day we'd met. No. I'd wanted him for years now, and I had him, right in front of me, wrapped in nothing but a towel.

You, Bastian. I want you.

In a second he had me backed up to the wall, devouring my lips, his hands roving over me like he was afraid I'd disappear. His kiss turned gentle before he pulled away to look me in the eyes. "I thought I'd lost you."

"I made a mistake, leaving. I should have listened to you."

His eyes widened slightly.

"Yes, I know. Admitting I screwed up is a big step for me. Don't make it weird." I rose on my toes and kissed him softly. "Don't get used to it, either. Because it doesn't happen very often."

He chuffed out a laugh, and then took my lips in another searing kiss that left us both breathing hard, my hands loosening the towel, which fell to the floor at our feet. He was warm—from the shower—I realized, and it was such a novelty that I couldn't stop touching him.

"The pilot..." I whispered, running my hands up and down his torso, skimming the pink scar, the edge of it slightly raised.

Another of those low, teasing laughs I was growing to love. "He's flying the plane, Selena, not worrying about what we're doing. But if it would make you feel better, we can move this to the bedroom."

"The bedroom, then." I stroked his lower back, then drifted my hands to his ass. His laugh turned deeper, with a hint of a growl at the end as we slowly made our way to the bedroom, my hands—and his—in constant movement.

The bedroom door was a tight fit, but we managed,

squeezing through, our lips fused together, his shirt hiked well above my hips, hopefully not flashing the pilot. *Who should be concentrating on flying the plane,* I reminded myself hazily. Being with Bastian, having his hands on me, his lips on mine, messed with my ability to think. So much so that it was another minute before I remembered he was deliciously naked, and I was...nearly there myself.

Bastian's lips fell from my mouth and skimmed my throat, his teeth nipping at my collarbone, before he paused, then sank them in, the sharp nip making my pussy wetter than it had ever been before. Ferocious heat gathered in my core, the kind I knew would coil and tighten before it released. The more Bastian's teeth grazed my skin, leaving trails of pebbled skin in their wake, the more I knew I wanted to know what they felt like when they sank into me.

He really was a drug, I thought foggily—he was a drug and I was addicted and didn't even care. He fell backward on the bed, taking me down with him, not breaking contact. One quick move and he was on top of me, his thigh parting my legs, completely exposing me. I eyed his fangs and pleasure shuddered through me. I turned my head to the column of my throat was exposed to him.

Is that really what you want, Selena?

Oh shit, I'd been so into this I'd totally forgotten the whole *I'm in your head* part of our relationship. He cupped my face, tipping it back to he could clearly see me.

If it is...I've wanted to taste you for days.

His tone, as always, was neutral, leaving me to make the choice. It would have been easier for him to take control, but leaving me the choice...

Yes, I thought. *I want your teeth in me the same time your cock is.*

Where that bold statement came from, I wasn't sure, but

tonight, I wanted all of Bastian Forge. I wanted his ferocity; I wanted his intelligence and his humor. I wanted to drink whisky together and talk about malting and fly to Scotland with him.

God help me, but I wanted it all.

You have me, love. All of me, for as long as you want.

His eyes flashed as he said it, his face turning leaner, the angles sharper. In return, I spread my legs and bared my throat to him, my hands lightly resting on his shoulders. *Will it hurt?* I wondered, his hips settling between my legs, his cock pressing against my clit, the hot, grinding pressure inside me ramping up inside as he moved against me.

No.

Keeping up the slow rubbing, he unbuttoned the shirt, exposing me inches at a time, until it fell open. I knew what I must look like right now: my hair a wet tumble of snarls, my face bruised, nothing to my name at the moment, not even clothes. But I didn't care. The only thing that mattered was how Bastian looked at me, reverence in his face as he reached down and cupped my breast, his thumb teasing circles around my nipple.

"Please..." I begged, writhing against him as my aching need grew more intense.

"I've got you, love."

I really, really liked that.

"Tonight, I'll give you everything you need."

Sliding his hand down my body, he positioned himself at my entrance, rubbing the head of his cock in my slippery folds, finally notching himself into the opening, then pushing slowly in, filling me up. My hips jerked up, impaling him even deeper, as I clutched his shoulders.

He lowered his mouth to my throat, licking a path from my jaw to my collarbone, then did it again, leaving my skin cold and sensitive. His mouth closed over my throat, then there was a warm rush as he fed—no pain; not so much as a needle prick. I turned my head further, giving him more access, feeling like I wanted him to have every part of me tonight.

Anesthetic in my fangs. Particular to some of the old Scottish clans.

I like the way it feels.

I did. Bastian's slow pulls at my throat kept in perfect time with him plunging into me; the sensation of him taking and giving at the same time was a heady aphrodisiac. My inner muscles bore down on his cock, the pressure almost too much as he slowly moved in and out, each stroke driving me higher, my hearing muffled, my fingers digging into his muscles as he rode me relentlessly.

This was what I'd craved, this out-of-control, on-the-edge-of-the-world-about-to-plunge feeling. My orgasm hit me out of nowhere, muscles spasming helplessly, as Bastian licked my neck again and picked up the pace as he fucked me. This one went on forever, until my legs cramped and my head was about to explode and every muscle in me felt tight and loose at the same time.

With a low growl, Bastian dipped his head and pounded into me, sparing nothing as he came, hot liquid coating my pussy, the insides of my thighs and the bottom of my stomach.

He dropped his head to the curve of my shoulder and collapsed, both of us panting.

There was no doubt about it: I was totally and completely in love with Bastian Forge.

And that was before we moved on to round two.

EPILOGUE

I rose up on my toes and waved to Bastian over the huge, boisterous whisky-drinking crowd, just as Seamus swept in from the side, looking like something out of a fairy tale. He'd opted for bright green attire tonight, from his hat to his shoes, making him look like a drunken, shiny leprechaun.

Bastian and I were in green as well, my lover's kilt a sedate plaid, my dress solid emerald, but the swath of plaid across my shoulder matching his. When Bastian reached me, he took my hand, grinning at Seamus until I kicked his shin.

"You look...festive tonight, Seamus," Bastian said, trying not to laugh. *He looks like a rabid leprechaun.*

Stop it, Bastian. He's so happy to be here. As am I.

"It's the final night," Seamus said. "Of course I look festive. Had to get prettied up if I was to hold a candle to you two."

Glasgow's Annual Whisky Faire offered a wide assortment of scotch whiskies, from newly bottled blends to vintages a hundred years old. Part of me wished we hadn't drunk Ambrose's last bottle, but that couldn't be helped.

Besides, we were just here to have fun.

The crowd parted as a huge pair of shoulders appeared, Cade's glowering face looming above them as he joined us. "Bunch of worthless humans," he growled, leaning in for effect. "Drinking all the whisky."

"It's a whisky tasting, Cade," I said. "That's why they're here."

True to form, Cade ignored me and instead gave Seamus's green suit a withering look.

"Don't be thinking you're all that high and mighty," Seamus informed him haughtily. "I've been coming here for forty years. They love me." Indeed, if one more person slapped him on the back, his dinner would probably come up.

Seamus set his hands on his satin-green hips. "I know a guy who knows a guy who can get us a bottle of McCallan. Fifty years old. Are you in?"

"Fuck yes," Cade said, loudly enough that most of the attendees in our vicinity turned around. Once they took in the sheer size of the vampire, they discreetly turned away. Seamus led the way, Cade bringing up the rear, and I breathed a sigh of relief as the crowd swallowed them up.

"Do you really think inviting Cade her was a good idea?" I asked, watching him vanish. "I don't want this lovely event to turn into anything...bloody."

"He'll be fine, Selena," Bastian assured me, taking my hand and pressing a warm kiss to my palm, his tongue making a warm, wet circle against my skin. My toes curled in my Blahnik stilettoes.

"How much longer are we staying, again?"

"A few more minutes should do it, love."

The last night always ended with some big industry announcement, but looking at Bastian in his kilt, I'd already decided I could read about it tomorrow. "Let's go back to the hotel. Seamus can tell us about it over breakfast. If he remembers."

"We're staying," Bastian told me firmly, wrapping his arms around my waist. "You never know when you might hear something that will change your life."

"I've had enough life-changing events this year, thank you very much."

But the past six months had been extraordinary. Between the Langston-Forge distillery and the Cameron Distillery in Perth, we'd spent most of the time flying back and forth across the Atlantic, balancing work with lots of play. Lots and lots of it.

My toes did the curling thing again.

Holloway's faculties were intact, and thankfully he didn't remember his kidnapping or the subsequent meeting with the Elder. We didn't talk about Brandon, and I'd almost put the ordeal behind me, except for the occasional times it popped up out of nowhere.

Forge was always there for me. Always. As if he knew exactly what was going through my head, and how to help me. Closing my eyes, I leaned back into him, my steady rock that would always be there.

"Here we go," Forge whispered, his breath tickling my ear. From across the room there was a shout, and a bright green arm with a dram shot into the air.

"Ladies and gentlemen, thank you for attending the fiftieth whisky faire in Glasgow." When the crowd died down, he went on. "This year we have a special announcement. Two distilleries, one in America, and one here in Scotland, will be merging. We will have a tasting of their flagship whisky tonight, enough for everyone, and it's on the house." The roar of the crowd welled up as my intuition tingled.

"What did you do, Forge?" I said over my shoulder.

"I'm back to Forge now, am I?"

"Yes, you are. What did you do?"

"I filed paperwork to make us the first transcontinental whisky business, the oldest American distillery." He kissed the top of my head. "And the oldest Scottish one."

The announcer hushed the crowd. "This is Alex's final batch, and tonight, he will be honored by those who best appreciate his work." The master of ceremonies lifted his glass high in the air, and the rest of the crowd followed suit. "To Alexander Langston, one of the world's finest distillers, and a legend in his own right."

Then I couldn't see a thing as the room went blurry.

"Ach, don't cry, love." Forge murmured in my ear while he gathered me close. "Your da was all that and more. But I have a feeling that Selena Langston of Langston-Cameron distilleries is about to make her own mark on the world."

If you enjoyed Devil's Cut, check out

The Banished Gods Series